Hurricane

A Strange Anthology

Writers
Ted Chiles
Max Talley
Chella Courington
Tom Layou
Matthew J. Pallamary
Lisa Lamb
Shelly Lowenkopf
Nicholas Deitch
John Reed
Christine Casey Logsdon
Dennis Russell
Silver Webb
Stephen T. Vessels

Art
Grace Rachow
Shelly Lowenkopf
Violet Sayre

Editrix
Silver Webb

Contributing Editor
Señor McTavish

Published by Borda Books
Santa Barbara, CA, U.S.A.
www.bordabooks.com

ISBN: 9781090540096

Copyright © 2019

A special thanks to Grace Rachow for use of the cover art.

Design by Angela Borda and Señor McTavish.
Kind assistance with image scanning by Mainstreet Architects & Planners, Ventura, CA.

Hurricanes & Swan Songs

A Strange Anthology

Table of Contents

Letter from the Editrix..6
   by Silver Webb

Where Have All the Good Times Gone?.....................9
   by Ted Chiles

Sitting Here in Limbo...15
   by Max Talley

For Thee..35
   by Chella Courington

Buggery...41
   by Tom Layou

How Mad Matt Won the Nobel Prize in Literature.......57
   by Matthew J. Pallamary

Nutritional Value..65
   by Lisa Lamb

My Dinner at the Boy Restaurant..............................79
   by Shelly Lowenkopf

Ghost Moose of Clary's Cafe.....................................87
   by Nicholas Deitch

The Third Hurricane..99
   by John Reed

East Toward the Sun..113
   by Christine Casey Logsdon

Closing Credits..129
   by Dennis Russell

The Hurricane: Mercury in Retrograde 139
   by Silver Webb

A Turn with Worms 159
   by Stephen T. Vessels

Contributors 181

Art

"Door" by Grace Rachow 8
"Junk Store Cowboy" by Grace Rachow 14
"Mannequin" by Grace Rachow 34
"The Roach" by Violet Sayre 40
"Shoes" by Grace Rachow 64
"The Proposal" by Violet Sayre 78
"Moose" by Grace Rachow 86
"De La Vina" by Shelly Lowenkopf 98
"Bull" by Grace Rachow 112
"*El Rancho* Steel" by Violet Sayre 128
"Woman, Spectral" by Violet Sayre 138
"Glass" by Grace Rachow 158
"The Star" by Violet Sayre 184
"The Magician" by Violet Sayre 185
"The Mad Hatter" by Violet Sayre 188
"The Trip" by Violet Sayre 189
"The Crossroads" by Violet Sayre 193

April 1, 2019

Dear Reader,

Hurricanes & Swan Songs was a collection conceived while drunk, laughing, and staring at a moose head nailed to the wall...as are many children, I'm told (conceived, not nailed to a wall). I don't have children. I'm a writer. I can barely take care of myself and the ubiquitous "two cats" that writers list in their bio blurb as a euphemism for depression. Although I argue that writing a good novel is more difficult than raising a kid; otherwise, everyone would have a Pulitzer stashed in their medicine cabinet.

Occassionally other writers, who are willing to forgive my lack of social prowess in exchange for conversations about semi-colons and Hunter Thompson, lure me out to socialize. Invariably it is to the same two or three restaurants. The places with comfy booths and tsunami-strong cocktails.

I believe it was halfway into a Hurricane and long past the point of dignity that I thought, "I should be writing these conversations down." I tried. You'd be surprised how fussy writers are about having their words stenographed and read back to them. Very fussy. So then I thought, "I should ask other writers to write their own stories about this."

I believe the first response was something along the lines of "Write a story about a bar? It's been done." Yes, well, perhaps it has. But not *this* bar. Not *this* Hurricane. Not *this* plate of burnt ends. Writers with busy publication deadlines stopped just short of suggesting that I should look into pills for my kind of crazy. But eventually my enthusiasm, if not logic, held sway, and stories began to show up in my inbox. Good stories from good writers. That's better than a Mai Tai.

And so was born an anthology about that restaurant, where nobody knows your name, and perhaps it's better they do not. An anthology about love, loss, and mayonnaise. Cockroaches, spliffs, and purgatory. Ghosts, both murderous and helpful, psychokinetic battles, and even a blind date among widowers and a not-so-blind date with Hemingway.

What was the name of the restaurant? Mary's, Perry's, Jerry's...it's that restaurant in your town, just down the street. And if you can't find it, look no further. Have a seat next to us, order a cocktail, and let the tall tales roll.

I would like to thank Grace Rachow for her art, and the writers who trusted me with their stories. It is no small thing. Muchas gracias to the Eminence Grise and Mr. Consigliere, who, with the sagacity of sun-bathing iguanas, have prevented many editorial spazz-outs. And, of course, my family in Santa Barbara, Los Angeles, Seattle, San Miguel de Allende, New York, Raleigh, and Colorado: You have not yet disowned me, and that is no small thing either!

Best,
Silver Webb
Editrix

"Door" by Grace Rachow

Where Have All the Good Times Gone?

by Ted Chiles

I walk out of Renaud's with my croissant to the shopping center parking lot. Scanning the tables in the plaza, I see a Ford Crown Victoria enter a handicap space. The approach is flawed. The left front tire crosses from asphalt to brick then closes in on the gray plastic-covered bollard planted for just such occasions. Staring at the fender, I wait for the inevitable collusion. I'm not disappointed. The plastic cover and the structural integrity of the car converge in a quiet bump with no apparent damage to either party. An older man, by which I mean older than I, an ever-decreasing portion of the population, pulls himself from the car. He meets my gaze with shame and anger. I smile and shrug my shoulders. From the trunk he drags a four-wheeled walker with a seat and hand brakes, opens and rolls it around to the passenger door. An even older woman is extracted and positioned behind the walker. They move toward the sidewalk at a snail's pace.

Choosing a table with a mountain view, I bite into the croissant. Heaven. I could be in Le Marais. A waiter delivers my espresso with a hint of condescension and again I think of Paris. The couple has stopped, taking a breather ten yards into their journey. They are dressed in a perplexing array of textures and colors, purple corduroy and burnt orange tweed, that must have been chosen at random. Sensible shoes sporting Velcro closures imply they don't care anymore. The woman leans on her walker, and I fear she might fall to the ground without its support. Her husband looks past Renaud's to Mary's Tavern, leaning like a man about to steal second base.

As usual, I'm dressed in a gray T-shirt, black jeans, and a black blazer. My moleskin messenger bag is also black, as are my Australian sheepherder boots. Today I'm wearing a black beret bought in San Francisco. I would no more wear a beret in Paris than a Yankees cap in Manhattan. Too touristy. My ensemble is not trying to say anything arty or hip. I just want to show that some thought and a touch of pride are present in the choice. I haven't given up. I'm still out here with some hope.

"Old age is hell."

I look up at the man and nod in agreement and appreciation for not having to hear "a shipwreck" or "not for sissies" again. They start to move on. I take another bite of croissant, pick up Pierre Lemaitre's *Inhuman Resources* and try to pretend I'm on a bench at the Place des Vosges.

My last sip of espresso is cold and bitter. The coffee, mediocre at best. Not that the French can make a café half as good as you find in almost any Italian gas station. A Cadillac SUV, the size of a baby whale, drives by, belching fumes. The label "American Riveria" does not apply to this section of Santa Barbara where I have come in my mid-60s. Recently retired, recently divorced or rather deserted, and in possession of a positive test for prostate cancer. The diagnosis doesn't matter. I am not going to let them cut me or mess with my already decimated testosterone. It may kill me, but I'm not going to let it fuck up the time I have left.

My plate is sparsely covered by pastry flecks. One can't call them crumbs because crumbs suggest more dimensions. These are flat. I try to find some meaning in their dispersion. Apart from a greater accumulation in the front of the plate, no pattern or message is conveyed that I can discern. A cool wind blows but the flakes barely shift, held firm by their buttery nature. The future still bleak and uncertain, I lick my index finger and clean the plate.

The older couple passes again on the way back to their car. But something is off. The woman who earlier held on to her walker for dear life is now pushing her seated husband. I hear a "wheeee." When they reach their car, he dismounts. She opens the trunk, collapses the walker, and lifts it in. She notices me staring. Smiles. And in that moment, she has shed thirty years. Her clothes a whimsical ensemble, purple and orange playing with each other. My hand lifts in recognition. She blows me a kiss, pirouettes, and gets into the car. The now not-so-old man looks on in smug triumph. They drive off. I watch until the car disappears.

Putting a dollar under the espresso cup, I walk toward Mary's only to veer into the courtyard. In its center is a dry fountain. Splashing water would be a welcomed counterpoint to the sounds of brakes and engines. I look at Mary's door, where sunlight turns the glass into mirrors. The courtyard bricks are a reddish pink that makes me think Florida not California. I start to count bricks. Stop. Look at the door again and think of other fountains. In Paris. In Milan. In Florida. I wonder why I'm stalling. The neon "OPEN" sign is skewed down to the right and feels more a trap than a welcome.

I remember another door, the door outside Debra's apartment. She was a born-again Christian, and in my youth they were more hippies than scolds. We'd been drinking at the Alpha Omega house and were both drunk. She more than I. We waited in awkward silence for one of us to prolong the evening or end it. She moved closer and hugged me. Our contours seeking to accommodate each other. Her hair smelled of smoke and Herbal Essence. I felt her breath on my neck.

"Ryan," she whispered.

My name a soft warm puff in my ear. I smiled with renewed hope for an invitation to come up and stay the night. I held her closer.

"Ryan. Come pray with me."

Now two warm puffs. I relished the feel of her pressed against me then kissed her cheek and walked away. Not because my amorous dream had been sidelined. No, I left because I feared what might happen to me if her God was up there. Waiting. What I would be required to surrender. A choice I revisit late at night after a third or fourth glass of Syrah.

    A group of six exit Mary's. Their step is quick, their chatter light and accented by barks of laughter. A tall man holds the door open for the others. They kiss and hug and separate into parties of two. I don't remember seeing them go into Mary's. But if I'd met them at a party, and later was asked to describe them, I would say they were young for their age. Youthful.

    I fail to catch the closing door. The dim lights inside mix with my reflection. I grasp the handle and step over the threshold.

"Junk Store Cowboy" by Grace Rachow

Sitting Here in Limbo

by Max Talley

It looked to be a horrible night. Michael wanted to stay home and listen to new Waterboys, Smiths, and Replacements CDs he'd bought. A December family get-together at Barry's Lounge had a four-hour migraine written all over it. Worse, even though he turned eighteen in three months, an adult, his dad had insisted he wear a tie and jacket. The "get a haircut" speech waited to be popped open like cheap champagne over dinner.

They bustled into Barry's entrance, the smell of the grill, all gristle and burning meats, the sweet tang of bacon quivering through Michael's nostrils, potatoes and onions frying up an irritating smoke no kitchen fans could conquer. The front room hung in a fuggy darkness that draped over diners embedded in their chairs as if they'd moved in and had no plan to depart until staff forced the issue. Slabs of Naugahyde rose to form shiny red booths embracing glass-topped wooden tables. Behind them, the walls rippled in bordello wallpaper filigrees. A haven for those uncomfortable in the present to languish amid the kitsch and disjecta of the past.

His father negotiated with a confused host. During the awkward interim as the family stood on display in the bright entryway—a kind of decompression chamber between the real world and the submerged one awaiting—Michael studied wall-mounted photos of the famous and the forgotten.

Yellowed pictures showed Ronald Reagan, Gerald Ford, Angie Dickinson in hot pants, and Ernest Borgnine rendered even more frightening by his toothy smile and wide eyes.

"We don't have your reservation," the pimply host told Michael's dad, "but we can push tables together in the back."

Michael's father palmed a twenty into the surprised teenager's hand—his first golden handshake. The lad grinned, his face a gleaming repository of all the pizza grease he'd consumed that year, then led them to the rear.

His dad looked distinctly displeased, as the monetary transaction hadn't improved their seating placement. Michael knew the signals, color throbbing into his jowly cheeks, burrs scratching inside his throat, a verbal castigation aborning.

"Richard, this is fine." His mother clenched his dad's arm as if a rail on a swaying ocean liner. "Look, there's Uncle Brad and the others by the bar." She remained an expert at distraction. Really, his dad just needed a premium-strength drink and he would forget the blown twenty until tomorrow night. Relatives converged on the table, the women claiming seats while the men stood and gesticulated with their cocktails.

The back room appeared vast and brighter, the noise of inebriated families and families of men who had no family ricocheted off the walls. A general din that rang in Michael's ears as timeless, the unimportant yet excited chatter that fueled human life, the world. Words that started as a mumble, launching you into the shower in the morning, then grew louder into a dissonant chorus before whispering nonsense and gibberish as you collapsed to your mattress at night.

"Hey, Bubba." Uncle Brad had a permanently reddened Irish face and gray-white hair plastered from one ear to the other. At times he seemed formed of dimples and bonhomie, however as the drinks progressed his countenance took on a demonic cast. Dirty jokes and questionable comments often followed. Aunt Judith generally kept him in line, and when she lost control, would flee to suffer the bad news in embarrassed silence the next day.

"Michael," Judith said. "You've dressed up for a change." She studied the tangle of hair descending to his collar like a scientific project gone awry. "You know, I hear crew cuts are coming back in style."

Michael smile-sneered.

"After your brother Franklin cut his hair, he got a job at that smelting plant in Lompoc, and married a fairly cute girl. Two kids with a third on the way." She squinched her eyes in what someone must have once told her was an endearing manner. "You could have all that too. I mean, you're no Franklin, but not every woman cares about looks. They want a solid provider."

"Excuse me, I need to..." Michael escaped. He plunked down at the end of the table, out of scolding range of his parents. For a moment he had clarity, full control of the garlic bread basket, and a quick gulp of someone's abandoned cocktail. Then his Aunt Lydia commandeered the next seat.

Lydia traveled alone. Various theories circulated about Uncle Jerry. He was a blubbering, incontinent drunk wrapped in adult diapers on a day bed by a dry bar. He lived in a perpetual fog, hopped-up on Nembutals and Seconals. He had a hoochie mama squirreled away in Ensenada, or possibly a pretty boy-toy in West Hollywood.

Lydia made her standard excuse: "Jerry's at his club. Some members meeting."

No one cared. Michael had come to appreciate the spatial void of certain annoying people, where their legend could exist ghost-like in gossip and speculation. Infinitely preferable to their physical presence.

"Michael." Lydia leaned closer and he breathed her powdery perfume, imagining entombed pharaohs. Her voice turned whispery. "I saw you stagger through my neighborhood the other afternoon." She signaled a server to remove the errant cocktail from near his plate.

"I was jogging," he said.

"You were weaving, all sweaty and disheveled." Lydia coughed into her napkin. "I'm happy for you to try alcohol in a social context. Better than smoking addictive drugs. But drinking in broad daylight?"

"That was me running." Michael only drank at family functions to make the whole shit-show tolerable. However, a penchant for bong hits transformed his practice runs for track team into a painful exercise of starts and stops, hacking coughs and near faints. Coach Schmilgin once waved a crooked finger at Michael. "You look more like a swimmer than a runner to me."

"My body type?"

"No, your red eyes. Too much chlorine...or something."

"Anyway," Lydia continued. "Hope they get your dad's order right. His temper tantrums are so tiresome."

"Uh-huh."

"There's much to be thankful for. Eight years of Reagan, and now Bush continuing the grand tradition." She squeezed his knee. "Who did you vote for?"

"Still seventeen."

"A thousand points of lights," she recited as if poetry. "Have I told you the Secaucus Waste Treatment Plant was named after my grandfather?"

"You did." Michael noticed his sister Isabelle sitting midway with a glum expression. "Excuse me." He hurried away.

"I borrowed some of your records, Isabelle." Michael stood awkward, hovering over two cousins. Family members dug into salad plates, the chime of metal against china.

"I thought you were all about CDs now," Isabelle replied.

"I still have my turntable. With CDs you don't have to change sides. The sound is better, a little brittle." Michael knew his sister didn't care about sound quality, he just wanted to ease into his topic. "How come you're not drinking and celebrating? I mean, you're twenty-one and graduate Cal Poly next June."

She beckoned him closer, so Michael squatted down on the balls of his feet, gripping the back of her chair for balance.

"Ever since I was sixteen, I've wanted to finish school and all the bullshit." She paused. "Now that I can see the end, I'm depressed. It's just, find a job, get married, have kids, settle down, get it together."

"Not sure I'll ever get my shit together."

Isabelle formed a wistful smile. "Seems inconceivable."

During the lull in conversation, they could hear their father griping. Not specifically at anyone, but airing his grievances over some food issue or slight the restaurant had bestowed upon him.

"Glad you're back home for a week," Michael said.

"Really? You almost never talk to me."

"Yeah, I'm still glad." He should have left it there. "I need a buffer, you know, against them." He angled his head toward their parents.

"So I'm your shield? You better sit down. The waiters are bringing the main course."

Michael detoured to a bar stool, but sat facing the extended family table so the bartender wouldn't hassle him. Instead, Uncle Brad cozied up close. "Have you noticed the stars on the walls?"

"The pictures? Yeah."

"See that blonde?" He pointed at a black and white photo. "Know who she was?"

"You told me last year."

"The first replacement bimbo for Suzanne Somers on *Three's Company*." Brad acted delighted by his pop culture knowledge, a drink propped so far up in his face that it seemed he might snort the alcohol.

"Right, okay."

"Well, maybe she's the second." His complexion glowed with intoxication. "Whichever one, I'd do her in a minute," he said, like it was a menu option. "Someday, my mug will be up there too."

"Really? Why?"

"Because I know people. People who know other people." He offered Michael access to his unused straw snorkeling down into the reddish cocktail. "And there's the big kahuna himself." Brad touched the photo glass with the gentle reverence reserved for a religious icon.

It displayed a bronzed man with a mushroom of curly hair sometimes referred to as a "Jew-fro" or a mafia perm.

"That's Barry. Our Barry," Brad said as Michael slurped up his drink.

Barry wore an arrogant smile, while his tan leather windbreaker resembled something James Caan might have sported in his heyday. A single gold chain lost itself among chest hair tufts; a giant collar splayed over a silk shirt. The dude must have been diminutive because Barry stood with his face sandwiched between two women's prominent cleavages, their unimportant heads cropped out of the photo.

"A real man's man. Drove a GTO, no, a '74 Firebird."

"When was that picture taken?" Michael asked.

"In the seventies, after he inherited this place from Barry, Sr."

"Is he here, now?"

Brad squinted with his nose angled upward. He appeared to be receiving invisible signals, taking weather forecasts, divining potable water sources, deciphering body language. "Nah. The staff's on edge when he's in the back office watching everything on monitors."

At the family gathering, no one looked happy. A jumble of verbal complaints haloed over the table. Isabelle held her face in her hands. His cousins grabbed at leftovers on neighboring plates as if some war-time famine loomed on the horizon.

Michael lunged over to swat away scavenging hands from the sweaty burger awaiting him, but he held no great appetite for it.

"You still banging that Asian girl?" Uncle Brad lit a noxious-smelling cigar.

"We dated. I think it's better we're just friends now."

Brad put his arm around Michael's shoulder—a bad sign. "You need to get on that and pound it into the ground." His eyes went misty. "Life is all about memories, thinking about what we could have done, or imagining a future where we'll do amazing shit. But we don't concentrate on the present. Hell, if I could go back to being your age, I wouldn't have said no to any gal who wanted me. Not the redhead wearing giant braces, or Katie with the lazy eye, or Sue who loved ponies and smelled like a stable."

"I've really got to go. Which way is the—"

"The head? In the main room," Brad said. "But that corner utility closet is a shortcut." He exhaled a foul smoke cloud then took his drink back.

Michael coughed before shuffling away. The utility room stored napkins, place settings, silverware, and glasses. A far door led into a long hallway where one could hear the conversational noise from both dining rooms and the kitchen and TV static jabber converging into a raucous din. At the end of the corridor he found two doors. Pushing through one, Michael encountered a fiftyish man dressed as a cowboy. He guarded entry into another seating area.

"You a guest at the private soiree, pardner?"

Michael saw attractive girls milling about, adults carrying

on with glee to a small live combo pumping out funky instrumental R&B music, and he smelled honey-glazed turkey, mashed potatoes, and whatever that fucking brown gravy was. "Yes," he said.

"You got your invite then?"

"I left it inside. Went to use the facilities and—"

"Okay, welcome to the El Rancho Room, buddy." His knowing smile wrinkled up a leathery face. "But don't cause a ruckus. Already had to give one joker the heave-ho."

"Course not. Thank you, uh..."

"Cowboy Jake."

***

Michael slipped into the El Rancho Room and hung inconspicuous, on the periphery. Everything looked cleaner, better quality. Even the air was sweeter; no one smoked. A huge buffet spread took up one side, so he casually drifted toward the deviled eggs—blazing yellow and red in their silver tureen. He devoured one with great satisfaction then reached for another.

"Careful there, son." A man in a madras jacket approached. Shit, busted. Michael hadn't seen a madras jacket since he was a kid.

"You don't want to eat too many." The man grinned. "They'll make you gassy."

Michael retracted his guilty outstretched arm.

"You don't belong, do you?"

"I'm sorry." Michael bowed his head. "I've come to Barry's over the years but not here. Didn't know it existed."

The man nodded. He had the look of a history professor: tortoise-shell glasses, an erudite quality of wrinkles on his high forehead, and the forgiving nature of someone who would never meet anyone who knew as much as he did. "Many people visit the lounge but don't find the El Rancho. No harm in you taking a peek then moseying back to wherever your table is."

"Dad, you're not bouncing the poor guy, are you?" A young woman appeared, gripping her father's arm. "I'll vouch for him."

"You know this young fellow?"

"He's a project, my new protege."

"Another one?"

"Dad, the guests are waiting for you. I've got this under control."

The man shook his head and wandered off.

"I'm Amelia." She took Michael's hand in her own. "Welcome to whatever the hell this is." Her dirty blonde hair was wavy, not curly, in a style straight-haired women fought to achieve, spent small fortunes on, but it appeared natural on Amelia.

"Thanks, I'm Michael. I was escaping my family."

"There is no escape, in the end. It's tragic. Have you read Rimbaud?" She leaned her head against his shoulder for a moment and then startled back up. "How old are you?"

"Seventeen, but almost—"

"I'm eighteen. How do you feel about older women?"

"I..."

"Just kidding." She lightly shoved him. "Grab food and join me with my friends. They're idiots but they're the only idiots I've got tonight."

Michael wanted to follow, but not too soon. So he lingered at the buffet, using metallic implements to spear turkey slices, and tongs to transport celery, cantaloupe slices, and bread rolls onto a plate.

Amelia waved him over to her table, an aircraft marshaller on the tarmac. Some woman in her thirties sat drinking champagne without joy. Two men nodded at Michael with surly expressions. He guessed they were suitors of Amelia who had fallen out of favor, hanging on for whatever leftover crumbs of affection she might toss their way.

"Michael, this is Chad and that's Preston. Their whole life has been determined by their parents just through naming them. Country clubs. Board rooms."

Chad frowned, while Preston roostered his hair upward with a hand.

"Jennifer's my cousin." Amelia gestured toward the champagne woman. "She's taught me about disappointment, sorrow, and bitterness. I'll be prepared when it hits me."

Michael studied Amelia while pretending not to. He took in the bump on her long thin nose, the unexpected wry smile that illuminated her features, darting eyes that occasionally alighted on something or someone then remained fixed.

She side-hugged Jennifer while shooing away Preston from leaning in close and kicked Michael in a teasing manner under the table.

Michael nibbled at the food casually. When he looked up, Amelia stared only at him, the rest ignored, invisible, background noise. Her gaze was positive, not necessarily admiration but of curiosity. A challenge for him to react, to respond to. Michael felt dizzy and butterfly-captured so he turned away.

No Amelias existed at his high school. She proudly wore a paisley blouse in the shank of the '80s over a long skirt that rendered her ancient, timeless, exotic. He could easily fall in love with everything she hated about herself.

"Let's dance." Amelia's green eyes burned into Michael.

"Sure," Chad replied, attempting to rise.

Amelia pressed his shoulder back down. "Michael?"

"I don't dance."

"Now you do." She led him to the corner where four couples were swaying.

The band played a funky up-tempo number and a black youth was sitting-in, plucking mellow phrases on a hollow-body jazz guitar.

Michael loosened up, the gulps of others' drinks he'd purloined animating him. Unfastening his tie, he threw his arms in the air, did strange jerk-like motions with his feet and legs, and spun around several times. When he paused, he saw Amelia contorted in laughter. Other dancers had given him space, perhaps fearing he would careen uninvited into their private dramas.

She approached, resting her cheek against his. "Okay, you're right. You don't dance." Amelia put his left arm on her back and the other around her waist and they slow-danced at half time to the beat.

Michael didn't complain, just focused on not crushing her feet with his clunky boots. Soft hair pillowed against his face and he could smell her, the facial moisturizer, a slight trace of perfume, the raw scent of youth burning at full velocity. He felt as if the Earth was spinning off axis and whatever happened, he had to hold on, but his sweaty hand slipped off her waist.

Amelia kicked his shin. "Watch it there, mister. You have to know the rules before you can break them."

Michael felt protected, hidden by and enmeshed within the music, so when it ended, he recoiled backward, unsure. Had the moment passed?

"Let's split a cigarette on the patio."

"Can't you just smoke inside?"

"Are you crazy? C'mon, dude."

Beyond the El Rancho Room lay a small brick-lined area encircled by a fence that opened up to the night sky. They both nestled together and stared at the stars, the creamy wash of the Milky Way canopied overhead.

"Like the song." Amelia pointed, then attempted to light her Dunhill with sputtering, failing matches.

He dug a Bic from his pocket and sparked it. She pushed his hand away, falling into him. Michael thought they would topple over but suddenly she was kissing him and he tried to relax and also concentrate. This was important.

In the distance on the freeway, he could hear the diesel horns of passing eighteen-wheelers, metallic leviathans trundling through their perpetual night.

Amelia pressed tight against him, grinding his ass into the chain-link fence behind them, all springy and squeaky. He tried to roll with it. Her tongue probed his mouth and Michael left himself, burrowed somewhere deep in the imagination, dark and shapeless, unconnected to his identity. He could live there forever.

Faraway noise tickled the air, came closer, louder, then displaced mass.

"I need help," a man shouted. "The parking lot. It's insane."

Amelia detached. "Don't worry, Uncle Saul."

Michael's eyelids opened to view an intense bearded man wearing thick-lens glasses, his eyes blurry and distorted.

"Will you help?" he asked Michael. Saul stood hunched in seriousness, carrying the aura of a Talmudic scholar, a probing intellect in his gaze, hands trembling.

Michael wanted to seem heroic—if it didn't involve too much effort—so he could return in valor to Amelia. "Sure."

Saul held what resembled a small walkie-talkie. He led Michael through the El Rancho Room, past storage areas, down unfamiliar corridors until they reached the parking lot.

Michael studied the scene outside with disbelief. Giant flames billowed into the sky less than a mile to the east. Not like a forest fire, but concentrated bursts.

"The plant," Saul yelled. "It's blowing."

"The plant?"

"The factory," Saul said. An explosion sounded and the ground shook.

Michael saw cracks in the lot's pavement, severely dented cars propped at odd angles. Pebbles struck his shoulders. Glowing ash descended like deadly confetti at a satanic parade. "I thought that was a residential neighborhood."

"What?" Saul cocked his head. "They built that plant at the turn of the century. You been away, son?"

The sky clouded with gray and black smoke. Anguished screams drifted over from the near distance. Basketball-sized rocks rained down on parked cars, smashing windshields.

"Those people are trapped." Saul pointed. "We need to pull them out between blasts. Just wait a moment." Palm trees sparkled into flowers of flame.

Michael felt numb. Perhaps he was hallucinating. Logic, order, recent memory. "So you're Amelia's uncle?"

"They call me Uncle Saul," he replied, "but who's Amelia?"

"The girl I was with when you found me."

"Oh, so that's what she calls herself now." Saul peered ahead. "Okay, let's go!"

They ran toward a pummeled minivan, the sky drizzling pebbles and fragments. Each of them pulled on separate sides but the doors seemed jammed tight. People were visible inside, unconscious or in shock.

A tremendous explosion roared and the planet seemed to tilt off balance, the minivan rolling over toward Michael, yet he somehow tumbled away. The parking lot lights died and he shouted "Saul" into an overwhelming darkness. No reply. Then a fist-sized rock struck Michael's head and he went down.

***

He woke inside Barry's sprawled on the floor. The power was out and the lounge lay deserted. Leftover meals sat atop server carts; some tables had been toppled. Puddles of liquor and piss became visible. Water dripped from the ceiling. Mice scurried about and two raccoons picked at a plate. He couldn't see a soul.

"Hello?" No response.

Michael's head throbbed but he pulled himself up. He needed to reach Amelia. And his family, what the fuck happened to them? Touching the walls to guide him, Michael set off through unfamiliar dining rooms, down winding corridors that led to more deserted spaces. He could find neither the El Rancho nor the rear dining room. Unseen things scampered about his feet. The place smelled musty, of spoiled food, rank perfume, and ancient regrets.

Finally he saw a glow and heard voices somewhere ahead. Michael dashed forward and tripped over something fat and furry that screeched. Again he went down.

***

Michael felt her lips against his and the nightmare ended.

"Amelia," he said, swimming back into consciousness. He kissed her, extending his tongue into her mouth, then tasted tobacco and eggplant. "Gack!" He pulled away from a woman older than his grandmother, her spiky white hair apparently manicured with hedge clippers.

"What the hell?"

"Listen, buddy," the wizened woman said, "you're no prize yourself." People nearby laughed. "We found you barely breathing. One of us had to give you mouth-to-mouth. I pulled the low card. You're welcome."

Michael rubbed at his itchy chin but a full beard had sprouted there. He sat inside a cramped alcove that contained a rectangular table with six others wedged in around it. "Where am I? What is this?"

"Welcome to the Gold Room," a senior citizen in a cowboy hat said.

The interior was indeed wallpapered in cheap gold leaf that chipped away to reveal the drywall behind. It had no door or exit, just a slot to pass food and drinks through.

"But I want to go back to the El Rancho Room. I have to find Amelia."

Cowboy laughed, the ballerina wept, and resuscitator woman lit a cigarette, her dinner plate a giant ashtray piled with butts. "We all want to get back to the El Rancho," said the buccaneer, pulling on his single loop earring.

"That's why I'm crying." The dancer woman's hair was knotted so tight her eyes bulged. "It's been so long, I can't remember what happened there anymore." She sighed into a gasp. "I just know I was happy."

"How long do you have to wait here?" Michael asked.

"Longer than you can imagine but shorter than forever," Cowboy said.

"I'm nearly eighteen. My whole life's ahead of me."

"Sure you are." Cowboy half-smiled. "And I'm the toughest hombre in Tombstone."

"I'm the best dancer in the Russian ballet."

"I sail the seven seas at dawn." The pirate yawned.

"And I'm a go-go dancer on Sunset Strip," said the octogenarian chain smoker. "Ever been to Ciro's? There's a combo called The Byrds."

Michael's head sank forward. "But Amelia's waiting. You don't understand."

"We do." Cowboy squeezed Michael's forearm gently. "See, we've all either been you or Amelia at some point in the past."

He dozed. Hours slipped by. People sobbed, told the story of their life, snored, broke wind.

***

Michael became aware again. The others bickered and played cards. "What do you guys do to pass the time, the days?"

"We tell each other stories, myths, outright lies," the buccaneer replied. "A steady supply of drinks helps. Mai Tais, Singapore Slings, Hurricanes, Scorpions. It's nice to be buzzed eternally."

"Is this purgatory?" Grilled food steamed up into Michael's face.

"Just a waiting room," Cowboy replied. He snatched three fries off Michael's plate. "You going to eat all those, son? Thanks. What about the other half of that grilled cheese?"

"Mannequin" by Grace Rachow

For Thee

by Chella Courington

Wednesday at Chaucer's I was digging through the fiction for a Christmas Eve book. Pulled Elizabeth Hardwick's *Sleepless Nights* from the shelf when I felt a tap on my shoulder. Startled, I turned to face an older man in a gray sweater, the kind with a ribbed neck, and a salt-and-pepper beard.

"What do you think of this?" he asked, holding a copy of Ernest Hemingway's *Across the River and Into the Trees.*

"Haven't read it."

"Why not?"

"Not a fan."

He frowned, and I added, "Too macho."

Chaucer's is a small bookstore with shelves so tight they leave little space for the reader. The air was heavy with perspiration and the frenzied angst of holiday shopping.

Searching for something to lift my weariness and take me to another world, I wanted to fall into a printed page. But the man beside me would have none of that magical trip, bumping me every time he pulled out a book. Never a sorry. Finally I put Hardwick back into her niche, tired of the stranger's presence.

"Where's Harry's?" he asked.

I'm tall, nearly six feet, about his height. He was familiar the way my grandfather was familiar in black-and-white photographs. A strong jaw ready to bite. I touched his arm, vestiges of my Southern upbringing. A gesture I make when not quite sure how to react or what to say. His wool sleeve scratchy.

"A couple of doors down," I said.

"Want a cocktail?"

"Maybe. Let's get a coffee first."

So unlike me. Agreeing to share time with a man I found intrusive. A man I wished were years younger. That I too were younger. We weaved our way out the narrow aisle past customers waiting for their books to be wrapped. The cool air felt fresh. We walked over to Renaud's, ordered, and sat outside at one of the bistro tables across from each other. He faced Harry's Place and I, the Santa Ynez Mountains. In the light I could see deep, leathery lines crossing the man's forehead. Traces of long hours in the outdoors before sunscreen.

"Cappuccino, nonfat milk, and an espresso," the waiter, possibly twenty years old, announced.

We tasted our coffee.

"Why are you staring at me?" he asked.

"You know why."

"I do," he said, sliding his palms over the table's surface as if smoothing cloth. His hands blocky and thick, freckled with brown spots. Like most of the guys I'm attracted to, he had dark, intense eyes. I imagined his body muscled and tan early in life when women and late nights were routine.

"Do you live in Santa Barbara?" I asked, twisting my napkin into a paper Twizzler.

"Just looking for a stiff drink worth a buck."

Behind him the mountains were patched in green. There were palm trees and blooming aloe vera. Tubular orange clusters dangling from the stalk. The medicinal plant with its healing virtue was not for me. My stomach was queasy, the way it groused when I took aspirin without saltines. Why was I sitting here with an old man from god knows where? A pretender. Why didn't I leave?

"Are we going to Harry's?" he asked.

"Did you win a look-alike contest in Key West?"

"I am Hemingway. The writer too macho for you."

He never broke cadence, never slipped from behind the mask. Played his role with absolute authenticity.

"You've been dead, what, fifty plus years," I said. "Why are you here?"

"I'll tell you in Harry's."

Curious, I finished my cappuccino.

He stood and offered his hand. I took it, unable to resist an hour in a bar with a man who called himself Hemingway. Better than a live manger scene.

He opened for me a door to what seemed like the 50s. Red leather booths with padded backs, enough room for parties of six or eight. On the walls the past lived in black frames. Frank Sinatra, Sophia Loren, Dean Martin watched over every whiskey and gimlet served. My man Hemingway was in his milieu. Loud and assured, he sat on the crimson stool.

"Two gin martinis with crisp cocktail onions. Coat the bottom with vermouth."

I pulled out my credit card to start a tab.

"My treat," I said. "So why are you here?"

"I need a drink."

The bartender placed two napkins before us, turning squares into diamonds with the Harry's Place logo of gold and red parallel to each other. Two martini glasses, frosty with condensation, appeared.

"Why are you still here?"

He took a sip and closed his eyes.

"Atonement," he said.

"For what?"

"Everything. I was a devil."

"By all accounts," I said.

"My sins were"—he paused as though standing at his typewriter, hunting for the exact word—"substantial."

"Women you loved and women you didn't love?"

"Precisely."

I considered myself somewhat of a MeToo, Time's Up feminist but sensed my body falling under the spell of a man who discarded wives and lovers. Being handsome and talented got him what he wanted. His biography from a long-forgotten literature class came back to me. A narcissist shadowed by depression. A genius who could not abide his aging body and loss of literary strength. At first he failed at suicide and entered Mayo Clinic. He was released and succeeded on the next try. A toxic male, the last man I should be attracted to. Yet there I was drinking martinis, believing then not believing that I was boozing with Papa.

"Tell me about 'Hills Like White Elephants.'"

He speared the onion and held it to the light. Concentric circles winding into perfection before he snagged it with his teeth. He gripped the bar and turned to me. I felt tingling warmth the way I do late at night under cover with my fantasies. His lips parted, ready to speak, but dangled me in silence. Uncomfortably long. I knew he knew I could be his.

"She wanted a baby. I didn't."

"Not fiction?"

"My writing never is. I was betrayed once and vowed never again."

"So you became —"

"— the betrayer," he finished.

I reached for my second martini. His admission hung between us. My breath was audible. He didn't move. The quiet became surreal. Finally, he raised his head, staring at his reflection behind the liquor bottles.

"I betrayed myself," he said.

His eyes lost their intensity, moist as though he were no longer dead inside. I reached for his arm. This time because I wanted to show comfort, let him know his wandering was not in vain.

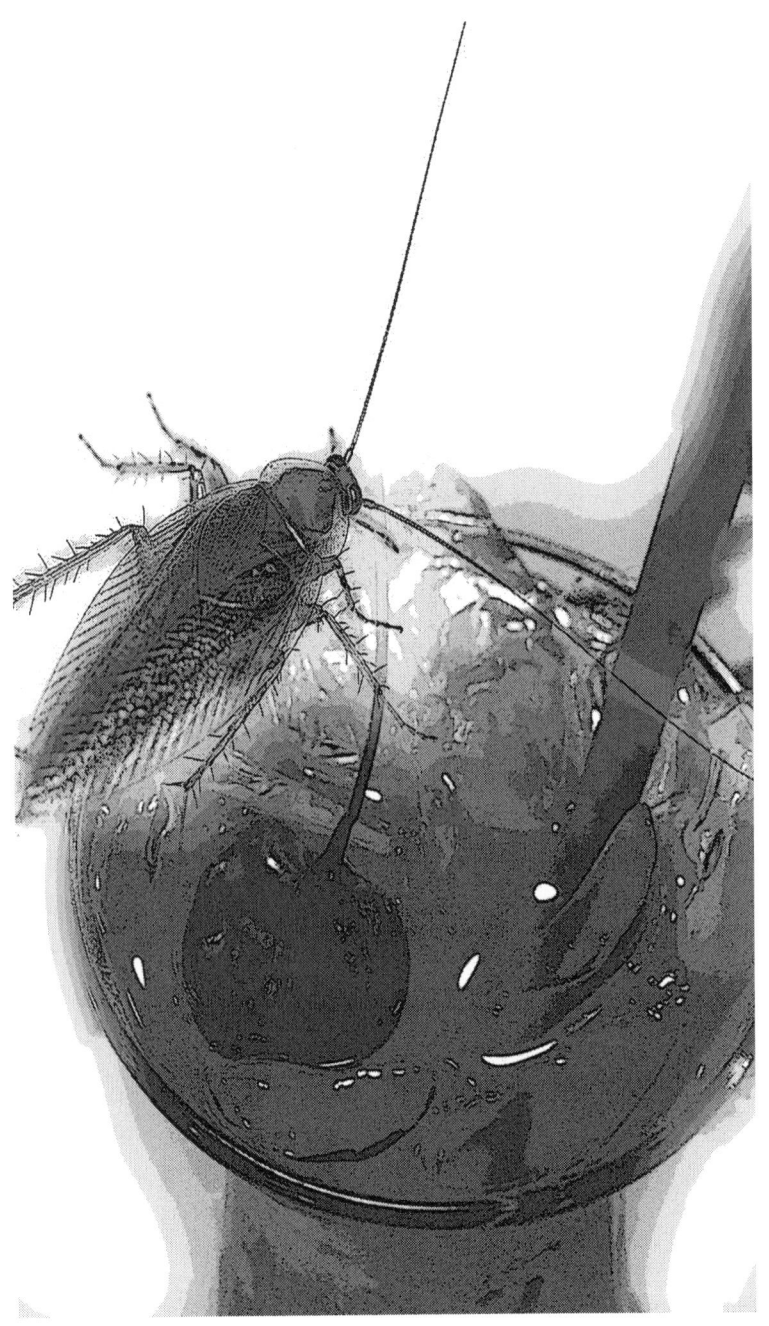

"The Roach" by Violet Sayre

Buggery

by Tom Layou

Don't get me wrong, I've always been a cockroach, I didn't wake up this way. But I've heard of that happening to a guy, here. I heard Billy Pilgrim came unstuck in time and something about seeing the best minds of a generation destroyed by madness. I know there was a guy named Ishmael, who liked boats more than people.

I only overhear these things at Larry's, I'm in it for the party favors. Larry's isn't some warehouse rave, but Hunter Thompson might say it is true behind some narrow door in all our favorite bars, men in tropical print shirts are getting incredible kicks some poor bastards will never know. The true brutality of living in the heavily abused restroom of a thriving establishment with around a half dozen shots in any cocktail is to be shared minimally, but I'll tell you how it works. Whatever hits the floor, is often recovered without prejudice. Whatever isn't noticed, is mine. I find my moment, dart out, maybe snack a chunk off a Xanax, and scurry back into my dark corners to wait. I tend to direct other infestants elsewhere. By killing them. With a slurry of the few chemicals I don't like. It's monstrous, but hey, free drugs.

Even for as early as it is, it's a slow night. That's OK because a fossilized dentist insisting Nabokov borrowed money from him spilled absinthe. I guess it's not early for everyone, though. Someone is giggling in here. I probably won't look. Jack is hunched over the toilet, like usual, at the moment doing his best James Joyce.

I heard a couple familiar voices rattling through the door. "I'm telling you, Howard, it's bullshit."

I'm always a little giddy when I hear Warren. The door creaked and two men entered, Warren in an anachronistic black jacket and purple sunglasses. His friend, Howard, was a larger man dressed for somewhere between the library and a safari.

Warren, in the purple glasses, continued, "His little jaunts to Santa Fe are pure fiction. He went hiking one time with a couple different coats and like three hats and some scarves to take a million selfies."

Howard said, "Warren, have you been getting into Ken's ayahuasca?"

Warren slammed a fist on the counter. "That is beside the point!"

The gentlemen went about their business. It sounded like Jack was performing a Triple Lawrence with a Dostoevsky finish, but they paid no mind. "He goes out of town, right, but he goes to a clandestine dental lab where he manufactures gold teeth that receive radio waves he broadcasts from his basement."

"Why, though?"

"The same reason he does anything."

Howard said, "He's weirdifying the planet through renegade dentistry?"

"There's a kid who's never left Phoenix, making a scale model of Manhattan out of fingernail clippings."

"So he does go to the desert."

"That was just so he can post them any time of year. Outside Boise there's a senior center where security has to routinely scour the grounds for improvised elk corrals."

"Elk?" Howard asked.

"They're teaching them ballet."

"You're full of shit."

"Said the man who brought me here on a ghost hunt."

"What about aging?"

"He doesn't. Look at any of those photos, from any year, look at him now, and say I'm wrong. He's got that Steve Buscemi timelessness."

Howard, washing his hands, asked, "What about Alfred, what's he up to?"

Warren said, "He's off handcuffed to a tree in some threatened habitat."

"You keep saying that."

"No one's told me I'm wrong."

I started to wonder if the giggler was alone when the lights flickered. A giant cloud unfolded from the mirrors and filled the floor. The place reeked of weed.

"Time," a reverberating voice erupted from beyond, "You will soon see, means nothing."

Warren and Howard stared at the unearthly presentation in the mirrors. A man in comfy-looking shamanic garb and a headband materialized. His curly hair was the same color as his cloud.

The visage said, "Nah, I'm just fuckin' with you, my brothers. But, seriously, being dead way changes your perspective."

"Ken!" Warren said, "Holy shit."

Howard took off the wide-brimmed hat and ran a palm over and down his ponytail.

I scuttled over by a trash can for a clearer view, and a better, uh, better air. Jack and I had been the first to see the former owner of Larry's appearing in the men's room.

"I know, right?" The apparition's hair wafted on the marijuana cloud. "Listen, I came here for a reason, though."

Warren said, "What's that?"

"I didn't die of natural causes in that jacuzzi with all those strippers."

"Well, Ken," Howard began uncertainly, "it was generally understood—"

"I was murdered in that jacuzzi with all those strippers!"

All three were silent.

Warren turned a red that complemented his glasses. "Who?"

The dead shaman's eyes flashed rage. "It was that motherfucker, Philip."

"God damn it," Warren said. "Then he moved in on Maude and hijacked the bar."

"And raised the prices," Howard said grimly.

"Seriously," said ghost Ken, his image beginning to fade. "It was way not coool," his words echoed. "You gotta get that fucker." The mirrors inhaled the weed cloud and snapped to reflecting stalls and walls again.

Warren leaned against the paper towel dispenser and whispered, "Motherfucker." He righted himself and tore the dispenser off the wall, shouting, "Motherfucker!"

It was a risky move, but I hopped on the cuff of Warren's slacks as he stormed back to the bar. The world blurred, a light-streaked tunnel, around me as we passed two waitresses.

One said, "When I'm having a hard time with a customer, I just tap into my greatest childhood memory, getting a kitten for Christmas from my Grammy. I feel the external tension melt and I know in this way, Stanislavsky is the key to good acting, and serving."

Warren slumped heavily onto the bar. "I want a fuckin' Long Island, Maude."

It was probably just the absinthe, but I could have swore I heard Maude raise an eyebrow.

"And two shots of tequila."

Maude said, "We'll talk." Glasses clanked above. "I know you must be having one of your, days."

"Ya know what?" Warren said, pressing his hands to the bar, leaning forward then back. "Just put the tequila in the Long Island."

Maude had tended bar since the Precambrian Era, but no one had ordered that yet. "You want tequila in your Long Island?"

"I fuckin' said it, didn't I?"

"OK, Warren, you got it," Maude said. The drink was made in an instant and she set it before him. "You want salt?"

Warren drank and coughed. "Oh, that does not bring the magic. That does not bring the magic."

"You want me to give you a regular one?"

"I'm fuckin' drinkin' it!" Warren swept a pile of coasters off the bar with one arm, a fleet of miniature U.F.O.'s bound for ducked heads, a few plates, and a receptive martini. Warren began to rapidly stamp one foot. I fled under the nearest table and walked in on four sneakers, two Birkenstocks, and an apology. A smaller pair of sneakers appeared to belong to a woman and I couldn't help notice socks and sandals crossed at the ankle, a gentleman who seemed like wherever he went, he was ready to be chill.

I heard a muffled voice way above the table top, "I know you really needed your laptop to finish the aquatic petting zoo blueprints, but my husband just called and, apparently the cats figured out how to work a can of silly string. It looks like Mungus may have eaten about half of it. I'm going to meet Jim at the vet."

A fourth set of feet joined the table. I could barely hear Maude whisper, "Is there any way we can ask him to make that a solo trip? I need—"

The socks and sandals uncrossed and I heard, "No, Maude, really, I understand, these are Olivia's cats."

After a pause Maude said, "How much alcohol will it take? I need someone to keep an eye on our young prince behind you, and I wouldn't mind budgeting about a gallon to find out what's crawled up his ass."

Small sneakers pressed to the ground as I heard, "No, I'm sorry, Maude, I really can't."

Maude's heels met. "I have bacon."

Warren noticed a space open up next to him at the bar and poured himself into it. "Hey, Sylvia," he said, "been meaning to talk to you."

Above the table top I heard the second man ask, "Is that what this is all about?"

Sylvia stared into her drink like she was flipping through a mental Rolodex of legal precedents reminding her not to get stabby. "Fabulous."

"I, er, read that story." Warren appeared to swallow a large fish.

Sylvia said nothing.

"Awful. Absolutely awful. Even a man with proclivities such as my own has no use for anthropomorphic mice on LSD. What the hell were you thinking? Who did you even write that for?"

Sylvia seemed to be thinking and as she looked up, Maude whispered in Warren's ear then walked away. Warren slammed a hand on the bar and followed. I heard his voice blend with kitchen noises, screaming, "Yo, Maude! Fuck you mean you wanna talk to me?"

I started heading for the kitchen and saw the second man rise solemnly from the table. It was Chuck, wearing a dutiful look, and he seemed to have the same thing in mind. I have my shortcuts and ways around the place, but I'm still a cockroach. By the time I got in the kitchen Warren was just noticing Chuck.

"What the fuck are you doing in here?"

Chuck glared severely around the tie-dye tapestry that hung in Larry's since it opened, lately concealing an alcove with a miniature office. "I'm fixing that glitch in the cameras."

Warren breathed heavy through his nose. "Why doesn't Olivia do it?"

Chuck said, "I have a security clearance," and dipped into the alcove.

"Security. Fuck. Well I don't give a shit about that." His anger was building. "And as for you, Maude. I don't give a shit what Philip says about all this, because I think you forgot to give a shit what Ken would think about you just letting Philip step right in."

Maude dropped her hands to her thighs with a slap. "Oh, for Pete's—"

"Do ya ever think about that Maude." Warren slapped a fork off the counter.

Behind the tapestry, Chuck said, "Hey."

Warren whirled the fork in a furious arc, jamming it through the tapestry.

"Jesus fucking Christ!" Chuck shouted, tearing the cloth from the ceiling.

"Oh my God," Warren shouted, "What the fuck are you doing back there?"

Chuck held his hands around the fork, lodged in his abdomen. He said, "I fucking told you I was fixing the camera." and fell to the ground.

Warren slapped his hands to his head and made rapid turns back and forth.

Chuck was still.

Warren jerked his head to one side and shouted, "The fuck! Did you fucking see that?"

"See what?" Maude said.

"Ken. In that damn hippie shawl he always wore."

"Warren, you've completely lost it."

"Lost it? I'm not crazy. I saw what I saw. What matters here is your bullshit, bringin' Philip's douche ass around here and Ken barely cold in the ground."

Maude leaned a hip out and put her hand on it. "I don't know how you say this shit. I couldn't."

Warren looked down at Chuck. "Well, I'm definitely going to Cottage Hospital now."

Maude's pocket flashed blue and she looked at her phone. It was the only modern thing about her. "Philip already called an Uber. Olivia and Gabriel will ride with you and get you checked in."

"That's fine." Warren closed his eyes and let out a heavy breath. "I'll ride along." Another long breath. "And you will learn, the sound of my fury!"

Olivia entered the kitchen with Socks and Sandals, Gabriel, apparently. Both were apprehensive, and Maude somehow shuffled them all out the back.

Warren was ranting, "Wherever there's an old hag pushin' around a guy needs a drink, I'll be there," and a bunch of other shit that kinda faded out.

I wasn't real sure what would happen after that but I did know it was time to peruse the men's room again. Nibbling on some anonymous-looking powder, I think I wound up in a

Buggery

K-hole for a while, but when I shuffled back in, the place was packed and Jack was gone. That often means entertainment, but when I made my way back to the bar I didn't see or smell him. That's not a cockroach thing, everyone can smell Jack.

Sylvia was in bad shape. She was standing where the bar met the brick wall, leaning heavily on an outstretched arm while she waited for her drink, head slumped on her chest. She perked up when Maude put a towering mudslide in front of her, dark liqueurs dancing on vodka. Sylvia turned and sloshed over to the nearest table where she leaned over a man, spilling on his suit. She fumbled with his butter knife before righting herself and marching backwards to the bar. When she bumped against it she leaned back and began to tap on the mudslide with the knife, hard enough to put the room in an expectant cringe.

"Good eveniiing ladies and g-gentlemen!" Her head lolled and she righted it. "I will now treat you to a lovely and jocund poetic work of an-nonymous authorage, first documented somewhere in the year 1941."

The nearest third of the room leaned in, a circle of indifferent madness beyond.

"There once was a handsome Haitian."

A woman seated between children hesitated and clapped hands over the younger one's ears.

"The luckiest dog in creation. He worked for the rubber trust. Teaching the upper crust, the science of safe copulation."

Before the room could hastily choose new conversations she promptly raised the mudslide to full height above her head and doused herself, snagging a few gulps, then slumped to the floor.

Howard moved to help but Warren came clomping in with Jack and three women presenting a tornado of florescent heels, fishnets, tight skirts, bursting tops, collagen lips, outrageous wigs, eyelash extensions, and faces in apparent recovery from collision with a swarm of rare and exotic birds. They were clearly strippers at least, no woman would be traveling with Jack and Warren in that condition without an exchange of money. Warren had his arm in a sling, hair standing madly in several directions, purple glasses askew. Jack's ordinarily disheveled clothes were torn and bloody, and there was an eye patch taped to his face. Neither could stand properly, weaving around and snorting as though suspended by a loose and rickety cocaine scaffold.

Philip walked in carrying a clipboard. Whether it was noon in a cafe or 4 a.m. at a manuscript workshop, he always looked to be asleep. When Philip saw the strippers his eye jolted and his face flushed red as he turned to leave the room.

Warren bawled, "That's what I fuckin' thought, Philip."

Howard said, "Good God. What the hell, Warren?"

"I'll tell you what the hell," Warren said, sidling to the bar. "Trashcan! Gimme a trashcan, and I want lots of vodka in that. The hell, Howard, is, that while waiting outside to be a third of the parties stuffed in the back of a damn Mazda, I fired off a text message to Jack, who was able to avail himself of my dilemma, for a fee. This good man here, this true friend," Warren slapped Jack heavily on the shoulder, "called in a favor with a certain mutual friend of ours to borrow a vehicle. On his way to our deal-friend's house, Jack saw a man stopped on a motorcycle.

Jack promptly divested the man of the motorcycle and followed suit. Riding between lanes and masterfully dodging through traffic, Jack was able to overtake my Uber, which at that time was following a pickup truck. With undaunted nerve and pure selflessness, Jack placed himself ahead of the truck and slammed on his brakes, causing the pickup driver to do the same. Jack himself would have been caught in the pile-up had the machine not miraculously bucked forward."

Jack raised his palms, and his good eye, in a beaming shrug.

Howard asked, "Are Gabriel and Olivia OK?"

"Fleeing immediately," Warren continued, "we ran ahead of the pile-up, where Jack was able to restart the motorcycle. Che Guevara never rode with such grace or courage!" Sniff. "After seeking medical attention, there were immediate concerns to be seen to and naturally we went direct to the Spearmint Rhino. Jack, who I assure you is the finest gentleman here, was able to find us the company of Candy, Majestik, and Chartreuse here. They could not be persuaded to leave with us until our character had been established, so Jack and I dedicated ourselves to that task, so that we could, in the briefest time possible, arrive back here, for my ultimate aim. Jack contacted our, uh, friend, again, who was able to convey us here."

Jack slurred mournfully, "But we lost Sugar Bunny."

It was the Rube-Goldberg machine of escapes.

Howard adopted his fatherly tone. "Now, Warren, I can understand if you didn't want to go to Cottage, but what did you bring the strippers here for?"

"Did you see the way Philip couldn't vacate the room fast enough?"

"They are strippers, right?" Howard asked.

"Yes, yes, they are strippers."

"So why?"

"They're the strippers from the night Ken died. I knew if Philip freaked out when he saw them then what Ken told us was true. I brought the strippers, Philip bailed, what's that say?"

Howard tugged his goatee. "Well, Warren, I see your point. I just don't—"

Nobody in the place noticed Alfred come in and squat down by Sylvia. "This silent spring," he said, letting go of her wrist, "will nourish my rage."

Warren hadn't noticed her on the floor. "Holy fuck, is that Sylvia? I was gonna tell her how much I actually liked that mice on acid story."

Alfred leapt at Warren. "You asshole!"

While they scuffled, Warren said, "Ask not for whom the bell tolls, man. I'm not crazy, but I am ready for a malenky bit of ultraviolence."

Philip set Warren's trashcan on the bar with his back to the room. I thought I could smell my roach poison. "Warren," Philip called, "Your drink is ready."

"Fuck off, Philip, I'm about to stuff this punk in his own trashcan."

Philip placed a hand next to the glass. Maude stepped behind the bar and appraised the scene. She sighed heavily and drank before Philip could object. Maude set the drink down and slipped out of of sight.

Alfred leaned down and got hold of Warren's ankle, pulling it off the ground. Both spilled backwards and hit the bar hard, dumping Warren's drink. Warren shook Alfred's hold, and as he flailed to right the glass, the pen from his pocket landed in the spilled liquor. Alfred grabbed the pen and stabbed Warren in the shoulder.

"You assbag!" Warren shouted. "That's a Mont Blanc." Warren wrested the pen from Alfred's hand and promptly stabbed Alfred in the abdomen.

"Shit," Alfred said, and fell to the floor, holding his side.

Warren leaned against the bar with a hand over his wound, testing his arm in different directions. He let both hands fall to his side and said, "Whoa-ly fuck. No bueno."

Alfred clenched his jaw. He didn't try to stand. "That's right, douche nozzle."

"I'm n-not feelin' right."

Alfred let out a labored breath. "Philip told me if you came back he'd poison your drink. The way you've been acting, everything you've drunk or jammed up your nose today, no one would question you falling over dead."

Philip was snaking his way through the crowd.

Warren said, "You prick," and snatched the remainder of the drink off the counter. Seats near the bar had been emptying and Warren wrestled Philip into one. Warren put him in a headlock and poured the last of the trashcan in Philip's mouth. "Drink, shitbird!"

Philip sputtered booze and slumped forward in his seat.

Alfred propped himself on an elbow. "I mean," he strained, "It was kind of a dick move on his part." Alfred fell.

Warren stepped back from the chair, wobbling. He looked around the room. "Well. I certainly have a few things to say about this but," he coughed and his head sagged as he leaned hard to one side, then caught himself. "I don't think I've got the time. Howard. You have to explain all this bullshit." Warren caught a table on the way down and something white landed by his waist.

As I moved to investigate, two women entered the bar, one a thin blonde, the other wearing a brown top hat.

The blonde spoke first. "What the fuck happened?"

"Well, Anne, I can tell you about everything—" Howard said.

"The bar is ours," Anne said.

"Pardon?" Howard blinked.

"The bar. We're taking it."

The lady in the top hat said, "I don't think most of these people even work here."

In this tragedy, no one saw me dart for Warren's hip.

Anne was adamant. "We take the bar. We get local creatives hooked on abominably strong drinks."

Howard tilted his head affirmatively. "Check."

"Then we mine them for their work."

Top Hat said, "It's perfect."

"Ah, fuck," I thought. "Mayonnaise."

Photo taken by Jan Stebel

How Mad Matt Won the Nobel Prize in Literature

by Matthew J. Pallamary

Matt, known as "Mad Matt" to his friends because of his obsession with writing, shuffled into Harry's clutching a dog-eared manuscript under his arm. *I'm never going to sell this piece of shit,* he thought. *Why do I even bother to keep submitting it?*

"Because you believe in your work," a voice in his head said.

It sounded so close and so real that he spun around to see who spoke, but saw no one. He felt a mild chill.

Fuck, I'm losing it.

He eyed the long bar and saw a slender, attractive, long-legged blonde at the end of it and decided to check her out and maybe escape his misery in her company, so he started toward her. Halfway down the length of the bar he tripped, feeling as if someone had stuck their foot out causing him to lose his balance. Floundering, he fell forward onto a bar stool, which kept him from hitting the floor, and by some miracle he managed to hang on to his manuscript.

He yanked his hands back, thinking it odd that the seat of the bar stool felt warm, as if someone had been sitting there. He saw the indent of two butt cheeks that did not come from him, but saw no drink on the bar. He straightened and glanced sideways, mortified to see the blonde putting her hand over her mouth to hide a smile.

A silver-haired bartender with a handlebar mustache leaned toward him on the bar. "You okay, buddy?"

"Yeah, sure," Matt said. "Sorry, I should have paid more attention to where I put my feet."

The bartender glanced sideways down the bar at the blonde and winked. "Don't blame ya!" He slapped a napkin down on the bar. "What can I get you?"

Matt snuck one last glance at the blonde, then said, "Fuck it! I'll have a Mai Tai."

"You got it!"

Matt took a seat beside the warm one, put his manuscript on the bar, and looked at the ass impressions, which looked really out of place. After the bartender brought his Mai Tai, Matt reached out tentatively and pulled his hand back as if burned when he felt the seat.

Still warm! What the fu—

"Drink up," the voice he'd heard at the door said.

He looked around again, seeing nobody, thinking he recognized the voice from years back. Too weird! He took a long sip from his drink. That ought to shut it up.

He finished the Mai Tai, feeling its effects calming him, and was about to summon the bartender for another when the voice said, "Well m'boy, try a Rum and Coke, my favorite, and maybe we'll see about getting you some help with that sorry-looking manuscript you keep dragging around. You look like a sad, lost little puppy."

Matt looked behind him, then to both sides and could swear he saw the ass impression on the seat beside him dimpling, like someone sat there. He reached out, grabbing at the air above the bar stool in a big sweeping gesture as if to pull it close and half fell over, looking up to see the cute blonde looking straight at him with a puzzled expression. She gave him a grimacing half-smile and a half-hearted three finger wave.

Shit!

With a short nod to her he sat up looking straight ahead, focusing all of his attention on the empty Mai Tai glass. He wanted to order another, but what came out of his mouth was, "Bartender! Rum and Coke, please."

When it came, he took an extended first sip.

"Atta boy. Stick with me. My friends and I will help you out."

"Jeez," Matt whispered, "not at the rate I'm going." He took another long sip from the Rum and Coke. "You sound just like Barnaby Conrad, that crazy bull fighter guy who started the Santa Barbara Writers Conference. I'd know that voice anywhere."

"Stick with your Uncle Barny," the voice said, confirming his realization. "Now drink up, m'boy, we have work to do."

Matt took another long sip, draining the glass, feeling the alcohol driving him deeper. He forgot about the cute blonde and put all his attention on the voice of Barnaby Conrad that spoke to him from somewhere inside of his head. Then he closed his eyes and abandoned himself to wherever Barnaby was going to take him.

"I know you write science fiction," Barnaby said. "Order a Vodka and Tonic, and Bradbury will come and give us his advice."

"Bartender!" Matt said without hesitation, "Vodka and Tonic, please."

"You're putting them away pretty fast there, buddy," the bartender said. "You sure you want to…"

"Don't worry about it," Matt said, waving him off. "This one's not for me. It's for a friend who will be here in a minute."

"You got it!" the bartender said.

"Listen, don't worry about what other people think," Ray Bradbury's distinctive voice boomed in his head when the Vodka and Tonic came. "Write for the love of it I tell you!"

Matt's eyes popped open and he half-expected to see Bradbury sitting beside him, pointing a finger to make his point. The blonde had gone and the bartender busied himself at a sink washing glasses, so Matt closed his eyes again.

Someone shook him and Barnaby said, "Are you paying attention to what he said?"

Matt looked across a round table at Ray Bradbury, who smiled from behind thick Coke-bottle glasses. To Ray's left sat Sue Grafton, Jonathan Winters, Dennis Lynds, and Ross Macdonald. Barnaby sat beside Matt to his left, completing the circle. They all had manuscripts that they scribbled on with red pens. Dumbfounded, Matt looked around, recognizing a meeting room in the back where they were known to have met. He had been there a few times times himself with his writing group.

"Don't you think it would be a better story with a female protagonist," Sue said as she continued writing in red.

"My Aunt Maude thinks it could be a lot funnier," Jonathan Winters said in an old lady voice with exaggerated facial expressions that matched the voice.

"It can definitely use more suspense," Dennis Lynds said in a deep, raspy voice. His eyes twinkled and a broad smile accented by his bushy mustache filled his face. He tipped his cowboy hat to Matt before going back to writing on the manuscript.

"If you really want to make it sing," Ross Macdonald added, "you might want to consider adding more noir elements to it." He nodded to Dennis and winked. "It'll help you address the suspense part that Dennis is looking for."

The discussion went on about scene setting, characterization, plotting, pacing, structure, and other critical elements of storytelling. Everyone had their own ideas, opinions, and approaches, and everyone made copious notes in red on their respective manuscripts.

"Pay attention, m'boy," Barnaby said, giving Matt another shake. "This is your big chance." He winked. "My money's on you!"

Matt shook more and felt himself slowly sitting up, like waking from some kind of weird dream. Forcing his eyes open, he looked up into the concerned face of the bartender.

"Hey, you OK, buddy? Want me to call an Uber for you?"

Matt looked around, blinking. He was the only one left in Harry's, and the lights were getting turned off. "Sure," Matt said. "Thank you."

In what seemed like the next moment he awoke in bed with a pounding headache, aggravated by the bright sunlight. His manuscript sat neatly stacked on his nightstand. He stumbled out of bed to close the shades and lost his balance, knocking the manuscript off the nightstand in a flurry of pages.

He stepped through the scattered pages to close the shades and shut out the blazing agony, then he dropped back down on the bed to stare at the mess on the floor. The red ink caught his eye.

He closed his eyes and shook his head as if to clear them and sank down to the floor, looking from page to page, seeing red on every page of the manuscript written in six different kinds of handwriting.

"Shoes" by Grace Rachow

Nutritional Value

by Lisa Lamb

Alice was nervous. Pulling into a parking space outside the restaurant where she'd agreed to meet him, she saw on the glowing dashboard clock that she was a full fifteen minutes early. Should she go in and get herself a steadying drink? Should she drive around listening to NPR until the appointed time? Or should she just go home and pretend that she had forgotten the meeting altogether?

If she did that, she could heat up some soup, drink a glass of Sauvignon blanc, and watch an episode of *Masterpiece Theatre* with her pants unbuttoned instead of making polite chitchat with a relative stranger. Doubtless he'd be affronted and wouldn't bother trying to reschedule, a notion so appealing that Alice very nearly put the car into reverse there and then.

But she didn't. She was not the sort to stand a person up; she'd been raised with better manners. Also she was more than a little afraid of what her daughter would say.

She could already hear Clara's exasperated voice castigating her for her cowardice and lack of gumption. Clara was very keen on self-improvement, particularly as it pertained to her mother, and rarely tired of suggesting the myriad ways in which it might be achieved. Alice suspected that Clara's motives were more about restoring her mother to a state where she could be comfortably ignored than any real understanding of what might increase her overall happiness. Nonetheless, Alice was grateful for the attention. Tiresome though it was to listen to her only child's earnest badgering, she preferred it to the sound of the telephone not ringing at all.

Clara's latest obsession for her mother was Internet dating. At first Alice had flatly refused even to countenance the idea, but after several months of being cajoled and harangued by Clara, it had just seemed easier to let herself be signed up for "Senior Mingle" than to continue her resistance. The name alone filled Alice with a sort of scornful despair, conjuring up as it did images of bewildered pensioners playing festively inappropriate parlour games. Oh well, she reasoned; she didn't actually have to use the site. Surely she would gain some respite merely as a result of her capitulation?

This proved a miscalculation, however, as Clara immediately turned her attention to pestering her mother with suggestions for specific potential matches. It hadn't occurred to Alice that Clara might also be able to search the profiles of available men, and while Alice was absolutely certain that none of them could possibly be of any interest, Clara was equally assured that almost any of them would do.

"What about this guy?" she'd say, pointing to the profile of some beaming, bald-headed hopeful. "Or this one?"

If Alice demurred, and she always did, Clara would castigate her for being preemptively judgemental.

"Really, Mom! Don't be so picky! At this rate you'll never find a new love!"

But Alice didn't want a new love. She had been perfectly content with the old one until he'd selfishly expired of cancer at the ridiculous age of fifty-eight. It had been two years since Jim had died, and Alice was still exhausted from nursing him through a long and brutal decline. She'd been in her late forties when he'd received the diagnosis, and she'd still had her youthful figure and a glossy dark bob. By the time he'd finally slipped away, his body shrivelled and his mind ravaged by morphine and disease, Alice had put on all the weight he'd lost and her hair was as steely as her heart. She no longer felt a part of the functioning, emotional world and honestly didn't think she could manage a relationship any more intimate or demanding than the one she had with the cat. Even that was a little tiring, with its litter box and fussy, changeable palate. But Clara was adamant and eventually Alice agreed to contact the least offensive looking of the prospective candidates.

Alice had not been on many dates in her life, and certainly none in the current century. She'd married Jim straight out of college in 1980; a trajectory more in keeping with her parents' generation than her own. But young Alice had not been interested in going to discos, backpacking around Europe, or hooking up with gel-haired Lotharios. An unpleasant, if hazy, experience at a frat party her freshman year complete with copious vomiting and a shameful stain on her underwear had cemented her desire for lifelong security and stability. All Alice had wanted after that was for everything to be normal. Safe.

She'd switched majors from pre-med to English lit., giving up her girlhood dream to be a flying doctor with Doctors Without Borders, and accepted first an invitation to dinner, and subsequently one for marriage from kind, plodding, unassuming, reliable Jim. Not a small part of her affection for her husband was the implied promise that she'd never have to get "out there" again. Alice was fully prepared to swap excitement and imagination for steadfast affection and the knowledge that he'd never let her down.

Yet he had. Here she was, all alone with nobody to clean the gutters, take out the trash, or warm her feet against on chilly nights. There was no one to nod and not really listen while she told him she was thinking of getting her hair cut short, or about that nice young man who'd held the door for her at the library which was so rare in this day and age, didn't he think? Jim had never been much of a talker, but since he was gone, the silence in the house had a solemn, almost hostile quality that was notably different from the comfortable, receptive quiet of his presence. Not that this made Alice any keener to meet someone new. She managed her loneliness by keeping the radio on at all times and talking to the cat who, truth be told, was just as disinterested in her day as Jim had been but had less compunction about walking out on her mid-sentence. Slightly less, anyway.

Alice looked at the clock again. She'd been dithering for ten minutes and was now only five minutes early. Deciding it was too late to back out now, she resolved to pretend a stomachache after the first drink and that way she could truthfully tell Clara she'd met the prospective suitor, and still spend most of the evening at home. Clara was bound to phone twenty minutes in to check up on her anyway. It was getting hard to tell who was the parent these days.

Pushing open the door of the restaurant, Alice was greeted by the hostess, a heavily made-up, mature woman in jewelled, plastic spectacles, black slacks, and a white shirt.

"Can I help you, hon?"

Suppressing irritation at the diminutive term of familiarity, Alice gave her a frosty smile and said she was meeting someone.

"Do you have a reservation, hon?"

Alice didn't know. She certainly had not made a reservation—wasn't that the man's job? She realised she'd forgotten to ask her date whether they'd be at a table or at the bar. Or even how she'd recognise him. All she could remember from his profile was that his hair was grey and he'd been smiling. Which, as she scanned the room, was a description that fit almost every male present. In fact everyone in the entire establishment, staff included, appeared to be well over sixty, which put Alice at the very youngest end of the demographic. Could it be that dating in the second half of life was actually just like eating at a retirement home? Unbearable. Alice decided instantly to leave.

Turning quickly toward the door, she yanked it open as hard as she could and immediately bumped into a gentleman who had been trying to open it from the other side.

"I'm so sorry!" he exclaimed. "I didn't see you there."

"No, no, it's my fault. I was in a rush," she apologised, eyes on the door as she attempted to sidle around him. It was imperative to make as swift and unobtrusive an exit as possible before her date spotted her.

"Say, you're not Alice, are you?"

Too late. Alice's heart sank, then lifted for a wild second as she considered simply lying and running away. But her upbringing pipped her impulse to the post.

"Oh. Yes. Hello," she said, stupidly.

"Well, hello there!" he enthused. "John Elliot. Good to meet you in the flesh. You know," he chuckled, "for a moment there I thought you were trying to stand me up!"

Alice didn't know how to respond to this glaring truth other than to titter weakly and allow herself to be led to a studded, red vinyl booth, tucked against a wall lined with flocked, velvet wallpaper (also red), covered in photographs of famous former restaurant patrons. An improbably young Ronald Reagan wearing a cowboy hat and holding a rifle twinkled reassuringly at the room over Alice's head. Next to him, several portly, smiling gentlemen sat about a round table, large, ice-filled drinks sweating in their meaty fists. They reminded Alice of her beloved father's fellow Rotary club members, and Alice was almost overwhelmed by the pang of nostalgia for her childhood that suddenly assailed her, followed by an acute and unexpected craving for a Manhattan.

"Have you been here before?" asked John Elliot. "It's one of my favourites. The food is plain but good, and the drinks are pretty strong."

Alice hadn't. The restaurant looked like the type of place

that New Jersey gangsters in the 1960s would favour. No windows, Tiffany lamps, bordello-cum-saloon decor mixed with mid-century kitsch in womb-like tones. Alice preferred modern, neutral-coloured, airy venues with big windows that took advantage of the Southern California sunshine. Also, she didn't care for "plain" food, which usually meant adult-sized portions of children's fare made with poor quality ingredients and copious amounts of salt and fat. Spare tire notwithstanding, Alice was conscious of her cholesterol count. However, she did feel encouraged by the thought of a cocktail, and although his choice of venue was not necessarily to her taste, she supposed John Elliot seemed like a well-meaning person.

Amidst some small talk and a few awkward silences they perused the drinks menu. At long last, after some time and a great deal of hopeful glancing about, their waitress appeared at the table side, gnarled fingers clutching a ballpoint pen and a small pad. She wore the same uniform as the other waitstaff; black trousers, black waistcoat bearing the restaurant logo, white shirt, and a small apron at her hips, but unlike her more regularly shaped colleagues, the fabric strained awkwardly across an exceptionally rotund midsection, giving her an almost beetlish appearance. Atop a head of wispy grey curls sat a black baseball cap, slightly askew, giving her a rakish look, and below it her powdered face was as wrinkled and puckered as Alice's fingertips after an overly long soak in the tub. Alice estimated her to be somewhere in her late seventies.

"What'll it be, folks?" she wheezed, and after they'd asked for drinks, intoned, "I'll-be-back-to-get-your-meal-order-how-bout-some-bread-and-salsa-right-now?"

She didn't wait for an answer but ambled off toward the bar.

"I guess we're getting bread and salsa," whispered John Elliot.

Alice suppressed a smile and picked up her menu. The selection was exactly as she had imagined it would be. Large helpings of meat, copious fried items, cholesterol-sodden sandwiches, giant bowls of unimaginative pasta. Even the salads were laden with heavy dressings, bacon, and cheese. Alice could not find a single item under a thousand calories. Her father would have loved it.

"So, Alice, what looks good to you?" asked John Elliot.

Just as Alice was searching for a non-offensive reply, a tall, thin, elderly man in an ill-fitting suit approached their booth. He wore a Giants baseball cap on his head and had an American flag enamel badge, the type politicians wear, pinned upon his lapel. He stood there, grim faced and silent, until John Elliot eventually asked, "Hey there, sir. How can we help you?"

"Give me a dollar," the man replied without making any eye contact. It was less a question and more an imperative.

John Elliot and Alice exchanged a glance. John Elliot clearly looked uncomfortable but nonetheless started to feel about the inside pocket of his jacket for his wallet. Alice wondered if the old man was collecting for a veteran's organisation or similar. He had that look about him, she decided.

"What's it for?" she asked him, pleasantly, more as a way of making polite conversation than really wanting to know.

"No reason," said the man. "I just want a dollar."

Alice's mouth dropped open in surprise and John Elliot's

hand froze in his pocket. A restaurant manager appeared, as if from nowhere, and gently shuffled the elderly grifter away.

Alice and John Elliot stared at each other.

"Well! That was certainly a new angle," exclaimed Alice. "The nerve of those people!"

"Poor guy," said John Elliot quietly. "How can it feel to be so desperate for money at that age?"

Alice had not thought about this before, having been left very comfortably off by sensible Jim and his prudent investments. Jim had always maintained that a man made his own luck and he'd brooked no patience for the misfortune of others.

"One Manhattan on the rocks and one whisky sour."

The antediluvian waitress had reappeared and was shakily conveying paper coasters and heavy tumblers from her tray to the table. Some liquid was already escaping over the side of Alice's drink and, anxious about the fate of her maraschino cherry, Alice reached to take the glass from the waitress's hand.

"Thank you so much," she gushed, insincerely, "that's just perfect."

Ignoring her, the waitress plunked the drink roughly down on the surface, causing even more spillage.

"And here's your bread-and-salsa," she said, dropping a plastic basket containing two slices of what looked like Wonderbread and a small tub of chopped tomato between the diners.

"Miss, I think we're ready to order," said John Elliot. But she had already wandered off. Alice was extremely vexed.

"How can they let her still be a waitress?" She exploded.

Normally Alice would consider it in poor taste to complain about the quality of service to her dining companion, but this woman was really beyond the pale.

"I know, Alice," said John Elliot, gravely. "It's a terrible thing that a lady of her years still has to work on her feet in a country as rich as ours."

Alice stared at him. Was he… admonishing her? Or did he actually think she was agreeing with him? Actually, what did she think? Jim would have said that the waitress must have made consistently poor choices to end up like this, but Alice knew from personal experience that some things that permanently altered the trajectory of a life weren't of one's own choosing at all. She paused to consider her position.

A silence settled over the table. Carefully avoiding John Elliot's eye, Alice dried the outside of her glass with a cocktail napkin before quietly placing it back on the table. Maybe he was right. She liked that he took a kindly view of people, but she still wasn't sure that he wasn't also making a sly dig at her. Maybe he thought she was some sort of self-satisfied matron who'd never known a day's hardship in her life. In some ways she supposed that was true, she had been well-cared for, but look, she had planned to be a doctor! She was going to fly all over Africa helping the very poorest of the poor, the neediest of the needy until, well…No need to go into all that, but the point was, there was more to a person than one might assume from the outside. Maybe that was also John Elliot's point.

Alice started to feel a strange bubbling in her solar plexus that she dimly recognised as excitement, an emotion long missing from her repertoire. Ever since this meeting had been arranged, Alice had been plotting how to escape it, how to return to her solitary lair, but now, suddenly, she wanted to stay. She wanted to ask John Elliot exactly what he meant and furthermore to tell him just what she thought. Not just about the waitress and the old man, either. There was so much she had to say! And she definitely wanted her Manhattan right now. Looking up, she was dismayed to see John Elliot, a small frown on his face, reaching straight for it.

"Alice, I'm so sorry about that spill, let me get you a fresh cocktail."

"No, really, it's fine, thank you," she said, holding on to it, alarmed.

"It'll just take a minute," he pleaded. "I'll go up to the bar myself."

"It's fine," Alice said, firmly. "Really!" She raised the glass.

"Bottoms up!" she cried, and took a giant gulp of the amber drink before immediately launching into a coughing fit. The Manhattan was much stronger than she'd anticipated, as if the vermouth had merely waved at the whisky from across the street. John Elliot jumped from his seat in alarm, simultaneously grabbing a glass of water from a bemused guest at the next table and enthusiastically thumping her between the shoulder blades.

"Are you okay?" he asked anxiously.

After a few moments, bleary eyed, watery mouthed, and not a little unruffled, Alice finally managed to answer in the affirmative.

"Here, have some water. And eat a little bread. Oh my gosh, I can't believe how wrong this has all gone. I told my son

I didn't know how to do this anymore…"

"Your son?" asked Alice, dabbing her face and nibbling on a crust of the surprisingly delicious loaf.

John Elliot looked abashed.

"This whole dating thing is his idea," he confessed. "He says I spend too much time alone since his mom passed and I've gotten overly opinionated and set in my ways. I think I'm just fine but he won't let up, so I gave in."

"Is that right?" said Alice, amused.

A horrified look spread across John Elliot's face.

"Oh, I didn't mean… It isn't that… Of course I'm very happy to be here…" he stumbled. Then covering his eyes with his hands, muttered, "Oh crap. See what I mean?"

Alice laughed. For the first time in what seemed like years.

"You'd be amazed at how often I hear the same thing from my daughter," she said. John Elliot looked both delighted and relieved.

"But frankly, I think I've earned the right to be opinionated on account of my age and experience." Alice felt a thrill at her own boldness.

"Brought you another Manhattan on account of the spill. This one's a little lighter on the Rye. Are you ready to order?"

It was the waitress again, waiting patiently, her pad at the ready.

"You go ahead, John, I'll make up my mind while you order" said Alice, taking a long, slaking, slurp of her new cocktail. Then, throwing caution to the wind she asked the waitress for a twelve ounce sirloin with a side of coleslaw and fries.

"By the way" she added, pointing to her drink, "this one's

just great."

"No problem," replied the waitress before walking away. "More bread."

Confused, Alice glanced across to John Elliot. For a moment she couldn't decipher his expression. Was it annoyed, or worse still, pious? Then she saw the corners of his mouth twitch and realised he was desperately holding his breath. They burst into helpless giggles at the same time.

"Cheers!"

"More bread!" they snorted helplessly at one another, until John Elliot, wiping his eyes, excused himself to the restroom. While he was gone, Alice's purse began to vibrate. Undoing the clasp she could see it was Clara calling to check up on her. Ignoring the phone and reaching past it, Alice picked up her compact and a bright tube of lipstick. She had a smile to repair.

"The Proposal" by Violet Sayre

My Dinner at the Boy Restaurant

by Shelly Lowenkopf

Ken Cole's sister swept her hand over the display of papers and photos spread over her kitchen table. "All this stuff. So like you. And so wrong."

Cole confronted a lifetime of his big sister's track record of right choices. "I want this to work."

Cole's sister offered a raised brow he recognized from the reaches of similar gestures from their history. Not disapproval. Meg didn't disapprove; not of him. Meg wanted him to succeed.

"And why Perry's, of all places?" Meg said. "Why not here? That's a genuine offer. She's been here before. She knows everyone. "We're glad to do it because—"

"I know," Cole said. "You're happy for me. Your entire family's happy for me. Means a lot. Really."

"But?"

"I enjoy details." Felt his cheeks begin to redden when he let on, "Perry's? My favorite restaurant."

Meg sent disappointment his way. Landed with a smack. "Such a boy thing, Perry's. Stiff drinks, comfort food menu. Elaborate ice cream deserts no one ever orders, except boys who've had two or more of the stiff drinks."

"I want this to go well," Ken said. "Not like my last disaster." Grimaced distaste. "I even went to New York for—"

"I saw the box," Meg said. "Not surprised you'd think to go to New York for it. You could have bought local." With her own, more emphatic sweep of the hand, she made an arc over the photos, pamphlets, and documents spread over the kitchen table. "Why do I suspect of all this—"

"Preparation," Ken said.

"Evidence," Meg said. "Except we're not talking courtroom trial here. You seem to have forgotten a vital consideration. Does Maddy like Perry's?"

"Why would you ask that?"

"You're lawyering up on me, Little Brother. Does Maddy like Perry's? Not a tough question. Have you ever taken her there?"

"We usually go to Stella Mare or Bouchon."

"But not Perry's?"

"Geez, Meg."

"Never mind 'Geez, Meg.' There are three kinds of restaurants, boy restaurants, girl restaurants, and neutral ground restaurants. Perry's is a boy restaurant. Have you ever taken Maddy to Petit Valentien?"

"Geez, Meg."

"Boy restaurants mean something different to a girl." She paused to let this sink in. Reminded him of earlier times, her how-to-get-along-with-girls lectures when he needed advice.

"You want things to go the way you hope, bring her here."

"I'll keep that in mind."

"Missed your true calling, Ken."

"How's that?"

"You may ace it as a lawyer, but in your heart, you're always conducting orchestras. You're a control freak in a tuxedo."

Okay, maybe Meg's approach had merit. He did over-plan. And she knew it. Still cherished the Zippo lighter gift from Meg, back when he smoked. Had part of the text of Occam's razor engraved on the side. *The simplest solution is the best solution.* So, away with the clumpy pocket file of honeymoon cruises, the photos of places they might live while searching for a starter home. The drape of his jacket sighed in relief without them. Meg always made sense. Give a nod to her bias about Perry's, but Perry's could take care of itself.

Okay, then. Nothing but the neat little blue box from Tiffany, containing the engagement ring. Hardly made his jacket pocket bulge. She might even notice, make the variation on the old Mae West joke, "Looks like you're glad to see me."

Hummed to the radio during the drive to Maddy's. Comforting, the way Bach got such a rich effect from a Brandenburg Concerto. No frills. All the instruments contributing.

Bounded up the steps to Maddy's door. Overcome with the effect of her when she greeted him. Even in a pantsuit, she radiated. "Wow," he said.

"You wore a tie," Maddy said.

"I wanted this evening to be special."

"Special," she said. Was that a flicker of suspicion? "You didn't tell me where we're going."

"Perry's," he said. When he opened the car door for her, couldn't tell from her reply, "Oh, boy." Or "Hoo boy."

In the car, Maddy said, " I wasn't expecting Perry's."

Fired up the BMW. Didn't quite burn rubber when he pulled off, but the squeal of acceleration sounded like a cheer. "Yeah, Perry's. Special place."

"I can tell from the way you drive."

Perry's. Generous sprawl of a steakhouse restaurant, stuck in the rear of a strip mall off upper State Street. Local legend had the mall named after a lovesick Italian stonemason, name of Loreto. Nice if true. Suited Ken's mood.

Gave his name, reservation time to the hostess.

"Aw, sorry, Mr. Cole. Should have told you when you called. We keep our booths for parties of four or more—" Stopped when she saw Maddy. "Miss Dunn. Didn't realize it was for you. He shoulda said. Happy to seat you wherever you'd like. So nice to see you again."

"Whoa," Ken said. "You never said you'd been here before."

"You never asked."

On their way to the booth, "Hey," Ken said. "You okay? You seem—"

"What?" she slid into the booth. "What do I seem?"

Slid in next to her. Bumped the pocket with the ring

against her. "Abstracted."

"That's good, Ken. Really good. Abstracted."

"Hey," he said. "What gives?"

Man in a dark suit, curly white hair, stood before them. No clip-on tie for him. Hand-tied bow. He presented a champagne bottle. "Miss Dunn," he said. "So nice you're here. The moment I saw you, I went back for this. Nothing elaborate. A California champagne. Our complements. I'll have your waitress serve it." Nodded to Ken as though an afterthought. Backed away.

"Wow," Ken said. "Champagne. I was going to order. And some shrimp appetizers." Motioned to the waitress. Felt that inner wave of confidence crest. On our way to Mr. and Mrs. Cole. Start of a tradition. Anniversary dinners for two, in this booth.

"That what you were thinking, Ken? Champagne and shrimp. That how you were going to start this?"

Motioned to the waitress again. "I get it now. Maybe I wasn't so secretive, after all. You read me. You guessed." He reached to pat her arm. "Can't hide anything from you. I really like it that you saw."

"Then let's get right to it, okay, Ken?" Withdrew her arm from his touch. "Fuck the champagne. Fuck the shrimp." Started probing her purse. Found her cell phone. "In fact, fuck you." Started thumbing a number.

"What's going on here? What gives?"

"You brought me here to dump me. Okay, I'm dumped. Now, I'm calling Uber to pick me up."

"Unreal." Felt a need to touch the blue Tiffany box with the engagement ring.

My Dinner at the Boy Restaurant

"Not unreal at all. In fact, all too real. A man shows up wearing a tie, brings me here, he's going to dump me."

Clutched the box. "Whoa."

"You already said that when you found out I'd been here before."

"You've got it all wrong. This isn't what you think."

"Oh, right. We can still be friends. Maybe catch an occasional movie or a concert at County Bowl. Well, get this straight, Ken. I don't want to know the reason you want to break up. I don't want to modify the personal tick you find so disagreeable in me. I don't want to have to find a diplomatic way to tell you how you fucking snore and you maybe ought to get one of those mouth guards. I don't want to hear that you'll always love me, but there's someone whose children you ache to father."

Maddy responded to a buzzing on her phone, began to thumb in a text message. "Yeah," she said for herself, "Perry's."

Couldn't help thinking if he'd brought those folders for honeymoon cruises, or the photos of possible living arrangements, things, they'd have gone different. But Maddy, while she sat across from him in the booth they'd been allowed to occupy because the management recognized her, she presented a different set of facial planes and an edge he'd not seen before. A stranger, a pretend Maddy.

"You've got this wrong. Things weren't supposed to work out with you thinking this way." Squeezed the Tiffany box with the ring. All he had to do pull it out. Plunk it on the table. Watch the sharpness drain from her, watch the fireworks of her understanding.

"Now it's my job to make you feel better about breaking up with me? Sorry, Ken. You're on your own here."

Felt his grip on the Tiffany box loosen. Placed both hands in front of him on the table. "Geez, Maddy."

Waitress came with an ice bucket and champagne glasses. Began twisting the wire on the bottle. "First toast for the happy couple?" she said.

"Wait," he said. Sat watching his hands for a moment, shifted his gaze to hers, then to the finger of the hand where the ring should go, where the ring would go, if it had a mind of its own.

The waitress waited, hands poised on the wire cork restraint. He sat, looking at hands, until he heard a foghorn voice from the front of the restaurant. "Uber," the voice said. "Someone call for Uber?"

Heard himself say "Here" in concert with Maddy. Surprised him. First thing they'd agreed on all evening.

"Moose" by Grace Rachow

Ghost Moose of Clary's Cafe

by Nicholas Deitch

His father would not approve. But then, his father had been dead for forty years, and the killer looked down on William Jeffers from a place of dubious honor. Thin spider trails laced the antlers, and someone had managed to land a bowler hat on the great beast's head, and at a rakish tilt. From beneath the bowler, Moose glared at him with familiar disdain.

Jeffers looked away. "I'm not in the mood for your bullshit, Moose. Let me enjoy my beer in peace."

The bartender wiped the counter with a slight shake of his head.

"Don't judge me, kid. A man oughta be able to enjoy his beer without some scornful Moose looking down on him with that damn judgmental smirk." He swallowed the last gulp and set the glass down hard. He glanced up, and the beast winked at him.

"I didn't say anything, Mr. Jeffers. But there's plenty of seats in this place, and you always sit in that one and complain about that moose staring at you." The bartender grabbed the glass and pulled the tap, amber bubbles rising to a foamy head. "And aren't you the one who gave that thing to old man Clary in the first place?"

Jeffers sighed. "You're new here, kid, but you oughta know. That's not just some rustic bit of bar decor molting on the wall." He looked up at Moose and tipped his glass. "Some would tell you he was a great Mohican Chief. A spirit warrior, with a slight chip on his shoulder." Jeffers took a long gulp and finished his third beer. "But Chief or not, this is my stool, and I'm not about to move my sorry ass on account of this goddamned Moose. He had it coming, and he knows it. I was there."

***

Forty years. Well, forty-two to be precise. He'd been to Vermont for a family visit, and he'd found himself traipsing the backwoods with his cantankerous old man. They were going to bag a real trophy, an elusive old bull that had become his father's obsession. Jeffers had heard the stories. Tales of the sightings, the near misses. The startling size of the animal, which seemed to grow with every telling. And don't forget the taunting.

"Really, Pop? A taunting moose?" Maybe. Or maybe the old man was just losing it. Whatever the truth, this wasn't just another hunting trek. This was personal.

It took them a full day to make their way in, well past the last of the cabins and lodges in the outer reaches of the Long Trail Forest. Woods that had been home to the Algonquian people for thousands of years. Woods that, despite the intrusion of the white man, still lay mostly undisturbed.

When they finally stopped to make their camp, the sun had already slipped beyond the trees. Jeffers built a fire, and the old man opened a couple of cans of Hunstworth's Stew. About as close to dog food as a body could fear to come, but the old guy loved the stuff. And Jeffers had to admit, when the can sat on a fire for more than a few minutes, the aroma could be oddly alluring.

They ate in quiet, listening to the crackle of the fire and the sounds of the nocturnal woods awakening around them. In the light of the flames, the old man's grizzled face seemed near to mythic, creased with years lived through many winters and a whole lot of mostly unnecessary tribulation.

Why, for instance, were they out here in the first place? Hunting some fabled beast that, if he existed at all, likely didn't give a fiddler's cuss about the old man and his obsessive pursuit.

"I almost had him, Willy." At the last mouthful of stew his father set the can down and nodded to the fire. "Three years ago, I had him in my sights, not sixty feet out." The old man leaned in. "I raised my gun and the beast looked right at me. He gave me a nod, and I'll be damned if he didn't smile."

Jeffers shrugged and poked at the fire. He'd heard this all before.

"Not a nice, friendly smile. Was more like a sneer."

"You were about to plug him, Pop, with a Creedmore six and a half. You expect him to wave and say, 'Howdy'?"

The old man turned to him. "I've been hunting these woods all my life, and I never once saw a moose smile. It was a mean smile. The kind that says, 'You'd better watch out, cause I'm coming for you.' I had him, I swear it. I pulled the trigger, and the son of a bitch just stood there sneering at me. And then he was gone."

He gazed up through the trees, at the branches that danced in the firelight. "How the hell does a bull like that just disappear? Unless he's a ghost." He reached into his pack and brought out his hunting flask. He took a long swallow and handed it to Jeffers. "I've tracked that bastard Moose for years. He remembers me, Willy. I swear it. He knows who I am."

"So, we're dealing with an angry, vengeful moose here, eh, Pop?" Jeffers scratched himself and sucked on the flask and handed it back to his father.

"I hear your doubt, son. But I grew up on this land, and my papa before me. He knew these woods as well as any Indian. And he knew their stories. This land has its spirits and its ghosts." He took another swig. "He's a trickster, that Moose. And I will not be made a fool. Come first light, I'm gonna find him and take him down, and you're gonna help me do it."

They finished the flask between them. Then they readied their rifles, tidied the camp, and unrolled their mats by the fire, waiting for sleep. It wasn't long before he could hear the old man snoring. Jeffers lay in the fire's glow, looking up through the branches at the stars that winked in the nighttime sky. And soon he, too, fell asleep.

***

The crack of wood broke the night, and Jeffers sat up, peering into the darkness. Beside him the fire glowed dim through the whisper of the dying embers. His father lay nearby, snoring softly.

Jeffers reached for his flashlight and swept the beam around the camp. Nothing but the black of night beyond the trees. He set the flashlight down and laid back on his mat, and closed his eyes, and tried to still his breathing.

An owl hooted far away. Something touched his shoulder, and Jeffers sat up. "Pop?" His heart kicked in his chest.

The old man snored on. He reached again for his flashlight, and shone the beam over his shoulder, and back through the trees. A shadow passed, dark and uncertain. And then, stillness. An odd stench in the air.

"Pop, wake up." Jeffers took hold of his rifle. "Wake up, Pop. There's something out there."

"Huh?" The old man sat up, stupid from sleep and whiskey, his eyes wide and hair gone wild. "What is it, boy?" He grabbed at his own flashlight and waved the beam about.

"Might be your friend, the Moose. Might just be a coon."

The old man was up and at his rifle. "Ain't no friend of mine, that one." He took a few short steps and stopped, listening to the woods. The snap of a branch some yards away. "Get up, boy. That ain't no coon."

"Maybe a bear." Jeffers rolled off his mat and trailed his father. The beams of their lights pierced the woods. The shadow crossed ahead, rising up through the trees.

"Damn. That sure as hell weren't no bear." The old man pushed forward with his rifle held ready.

Jeffers stepped into his father's tracks, the air around them rank and wild. Beside the trail, the world seemed to fall away.

Another crack of wood, this one to their left. Jeffers swung around and caught the beast in his light, huge antlers and nostrils flared, standing like a man.

"There he is, Pop. God almighty, look at him!"

"Son of a bitch, it's you!" The old man stepped forward and fired into the trees. "Gotcha!" He ran toward the kill, with Jeffers close behind. They shined their lights where the beast should have fallen. Behold, a steaming pile of moose dung glistened in the torchlight.

The old man stood trembling. "Well, goddammit. I ain't never in my life—"

A rumble through the dark, and before Jeffers could think, the beast lunged at his father, catching him in those huge antlers. With a twist of its neck the creature flung the old man through the air, landing him hard against a tree with a thud. The beast turned on Jeffers, who stood there dumb with disbelief.

"What the hell are you?" His heart pounded in his ears.

The great Moose bent down and wrenched its antlers from side to side, peering into Jeffers' face. And then to Jeffers' utter disbelief, the damned thing grinned at him, teeth big and yellow, nostrils flared, those great hoofs cutting at the earth through a deep, bellowing groan.

Jeffers raised his gun and fired.

***

It took two days, with the help of Wilderness Rescue and a few puzzled friends, for Jeffers to extract his dead father, and the carcass of the huge bull moose.

The day after the funeral, Jeffers drove the old man's '68 Cutlass to Northern Reaches Taxidermy. The man brought him to the tarp-covered trophy at rest on a table. "That's gotta be the biggest moose I've ever seen, and damn sure the oldest."

He pulled the tarp off, and Jeffers stared into the face of his father's nemesis. He held his breath, half expecting the thing to grin at him with gnashing teeth.

"Been shot more than once. Your's went through the heart. There was an old shoulder wound that healed badly. And... I found an arrowhead in a haunch. I'd swear it was Mohican, if I didn't know better." The man turned the mount in admiration of his work. "This one walked the earth for a hell of a long time."

Jeffers wasn't listening. He stared into the eye of the great Moose, and he could swear the creature stared back. He wanted to burn the thing in his mother's backyard. He wanted to get the hell out of Vermont and back to the sunny reaches of Southern California.

He tried to write a check, but the man refused. "Your dad paid for this mount three years ago. Real sorry, son, but I guess he finally got his kill." The man produced a bill of sale, along with some instructions for the shipping. "Says here that the specimen is intended as a peace offering. Some fellow named Clary McDowell. Owns a bar in Santa Barbara."

"I worked at Clary's, while I finished school. My dad arranged it." Jeffers took the bill and stared at the notations in his father's hand.

"Well, I guess they were friends. Did a lot of hunting together. Had some sorta falling out, and this was meant to set it right." The fellow nodded. "Oh, heya. I think you ought to have this." He reached into a pocket and held out an arrowhead. "This belongs to you now. An unusual find these days, for sure. I'd bet that handwork is near to three hundred years old."

Jeffers studied the artifact. Chipped quartzite, about two inches long, shaped to a knife's edge by a skilled hand. He slipped the arrowhead into his pocket and thanked the man.

***

How does one transport a huge moose head three thousand miles across the country? Jeffers considered his options and decided to take the old man's Cutlass and deliver the Moose himself.

It took ten bungee cords to strap the thing down. He'd started on the roof of the car, but the stability was problematic, and even seemed a bit disrespectful. He propped the thing against the windshield and found that he could see quite well from the driver's side with only a slight stoop at the wheel to peer beneath an antler.

Jeffers got out of the car and stepped back to admire his rigging. The old man had kept the Cutlass in fine shape, and the deep metallic blue of the finish glistened in the noonday sun. Although the arrangement imbued the trophy with an almost proper touch of nobility, Jeffers worried. The spectacle of the world's largest hood ornament might cause some unintended distraction for the weary highway traveler, so he wrapped the thing in canvas. Early the next morning he pulled onto the highway, heading for the California coast.

About fourteen hundred miles into the journey, Jeffers began to notice a heightened level of gawking and bewildered stares. The tarp had come loose, and he could hear the canvas flapping on the car top. From a distance, the effect was startling, of a great caped Moose soaring across the waving fields of the Nebraska prairie at seventy miles per hour.

The Lincoln County Sheriff was not impressed. "What

the hell are you thinking, son, parading this thing down the highway?" They stood on the shoulder, the patrol car's lights flashing red and blue. "You're scaring people. And someone's gonna crash and burn on account of this fool-ishness."

Jeffers frowned at the Moose. He had fastened that tarp with slip knots, and tested the rigging. He pulled the tarp tight over the face of the beast, but he could feel those eyes glaring at him through the canvas. Something burned in the pocket of his pants.

"What the hell?" He reached in and took out the arrowhead. It felt hot in his palm.

"Let me see that, son." The sheriff leaned in close. "That's a real beauty, that is. You best not show that around. Some take offense at the pilfering of artifacts." The sheriff sent him on his way with a caution. "Do me a favor and stay off the main highway for a bit, will ya."

He made California by nightfall of the fourth day. By the time he arrived at Clary's, it was almost midnight, but the place was still hopping. He parked out back and went in through the kitchen, straight for Clary's office, and knocked on the door.

Clary looked up from his desk and brightened. He rose and came around. "William, it's good to see you, son. I was sorry to hear about your father. And now I'm sorry that we never did sort things out."

Jeffers nodded. "Yes, sir. But I've got something for you. Something my pop wanted you to have."

They walked out back and stood in front of the Cutlass, and Jeffers pulled the canvas away. Clary caught his breath, and he almost fell over.

"God almighty, that's him. That's the Ghost. I'd swear it, though it don't seem possible." Clary stepped back and sat on a crate. "He's even bigger than I remember."

"Why'd you call him a ghost?" Jeffers frowned.

Clary gazed at the mount and then he pushed himself up and stepped closer. "We'd heard the stories, your pop and me, about a great spirit Moose. Some said he was a chief, but what the hell did we know? We were just teenagers. Your pop thought it was nonsense, but I convinced him that we had to find out for ourselves."

"Five days we tracked him, but we couldn't catch a glimpse. He seemed always just beyond our reach. On the last morning, I'd finished my business, and I was buckling my pants, and I looked up and there he was, drinking at a stream. The biggest goddamned Moose I ever saw. My heart was pounding so hard I thought he might hear it. I grabbed my rifle and got a bead on him and I was about to take the shot when your pop came tromping through the bush and walked right into me. My gun went off, and the moose just vanished, like mist in the sunlight. I was so mad at your pop, I let him have it, with a hard right to his jaw." Clary rubbed his fist absently. "I still feel badly about it." He sighed. "Hitler was causing his havoc, and a few months later I was on a steamer heading for France. Your pop was sent to the Pacific, and we never saw each other again."

Clary reached for the Moose, and with a kind of reverence he ran his hand along the beast's great muzzle. "Your pop was a good friend, and I'm sorry for your loss, son."

Jeffers nodded. "Yes, sir. Thank you. I guess he became a believer, because he's been hunting this Moose for as long as I can remember. Seems he was hunting it for you."

***

Jeffers turned to look up at the mount on the wall, the Moose there glaring at him. Rakish bowler and cobwebs. "Forty years I been coming to Clary's. Forty years of attitude from a dead Moose."

The bartender frowned at him and puzzled. "Seems sad, such a noble animal should have a fate like this. Maybe you're feeling guilty, Mr. Jeffers."

"What do you mean, kid? Don't seem so bad to me, a place of honor in a fine establishment like Clary's." But Jeffers looked again at the Moose, and considered the comment further. He set his glass down and grabbed a towel from the bar. "Maybe you're right, son. After all these years, I suppose a little respect is due."

Jeffers stepped onto a chair and gave the beast a good whisking, and even wiped the cobwebs from the antlers. He stopped to pat the muzzle, and then reached up to straighten the bowler to a more dignified line.

He returned to his stool and pulled out the shard of stone that hung from a chain around his neck. He clenched it in his fist, and raised his drink and nodded at the great Moose. "Let's call it a truce, old fella." He swallowed the last of his beer and set the glass down. His hand burned, and he opened his fist to see the flesh seared and tender, the shape of the arrowhead emblazoned on the skin of his palm.

The bartender reached to refill his glass, but stopped, with a look of doubt. "Mr. Jeffers, you can laugh if you want, but I'd swear that Moose just smiled."

"Look away, kid, and don't pay him any mind." Jeffers handed him the empty glass. "Just step back from the bar, and look the other way."

"De La Vina" by Shelly Lowenkopf

The Third Hurricane

by John Reed

The phone that could not ring—rang at 11:03 that night. At that moment, Andy Culver believed he'd finally gone insane. A phone with no battery could not ring, at least not in the real world. He threw off his blue tarp and sat up trembling in the darkness under the bridge.

Two rings. Three.

No, he would not answer a phone that was not ringing, would not give in to his insanity. But what if it was her?

He fumbled in his backpack, found it, and answered on the fourth ring. "Hello?"

Mary's voice was unmistakable. "Come to Harry's. Midnight."

A blue glow blossomed around him, giving the concrete arch of the highway bridge above him the look of a deep-sea grotto. Weeds waved like sea grass. He shook his head, trying to clear the images away. It was no use, the madness had him, would never let him go. His recurring dream came back:

Nightfall on Hendry's beach in Santa Barbara, the ocean calm under a gibbous moon. A woman walks toward him out of the mist. She is so beautiful—teal green eyes—he cannot believe she is real. A blast of wind knocks him down. The woman is gone. Waves thunder over him, he's fighting for breath. His mother's face appears and floats toward him out of the depths. He is underwater fighting to breathe.

He screamed into the phone, "You're not real . . . wait a minute, don't hang up."

The screen went black.

The blue light faded. Darkness again enveloped his hideout under the bridge. He sat in the dirt, stunned. A voice from a dead phone. A madman's dream. Still he fought the idea that Mary was somehow a figment of his imagination. She felt as real as any woman ever could. Still, their first meeting had an other-worldly feel.

He had been walking along the beach on the fifth anniversary of his mother's death, carrying, as he did every year, a white rose. Her plane went down off the Santa Barbara coast on her first solo flight. They found the wreckage, but never found his mother's body. A recurring nightmare tortured him: She rises from the depths, eyes wide, hands reaching for him. He had never again ventured into the water.

Each year, on the anniversary of her death, he tossed a rose onto the water, a memorial service.

The night Mary appeared, he had tossed the rose onto the water as usual, but this time a sudden wind came up from the west, pushed the flower back onto the beach. He sat down on the sand, face in his hands, wallowing in sadness. A loser who couldn't even honor the memory of his dead mother.

A flash of white near a rocky outcropping. The woman walking toward him seemed almost borne on the wind. Her red hair and long white dress flowed behind her. A striped scarf that reminded Andy of Dr. Who, fluttered around her shoulders. He stared at her, mesmerized by the light in her green eyes.

She pointed at the rose. "I don't suppose that's for me."

He held it out to her. "It is now."

Their hands touched as he handed her the flower. Her fingers felt warm. "What are you doing down here at night?" he asked.

"I come here sometimes when I need to," she said. "Tonight, I need to."

Their attraction was instantaneous. It grew into a tumultuous six-month affair that changed Andy's life. He cast off his loser image, took a new job cooking at a Mexican restaurant on State Street. His nightmares faded. Then one night Mary disappeared and Andy was a loser again. His long decline, his desperate sadness at his loss, drove him at last to madness, left him homeless, sleeping under a bridge. He grew to hate her—she had destroyed his life. Still, as he sat alone under the bridge, all he could think of was: *Harry's bar in an hour.*

He jammed his blue tarp into a garbage bag along with all his worldly possessions, some stale cookies, empty cans, dirty clothes. The only real thing of value, the blue and green Dr. Who scarf Mary had left behind, Andy wrapped around his shoulders. He picked up his bag and scrambled out from under the bridge.

The street lights along Las Positas, a main drag in Santa Barbara, cast a sickly, greenish glow in the fog around him. He fought his way through trash and knee-high weeds. Two ragged figures crept toward him, street people. Their faces were concealed by silver masks, giving them a robotic look. A blue aura surrounded them, burning holes in the fog. Andy put down his bag and balled his fists.

Before he could react, they were on him, kicking and punching. The taller one produced a knife, held it low.

"Careful, man," his partner said,

The knife-wielder swung the blade in lazy circles. "You heard what the bitch said, 'Make him bleed.'"

Andy raised his knee to block the knife, felt a sudden flash of pain. Blood trickled down his leg. He fell to the ground. Feet and fists rained down on him. He wrapped his arms around his head and braced for death. The blows stopped. He sat up clutching his leg, grimacing with pain. The two men ran away toward Las Positas. The aura surrounding them shrank to a star point and vanished in the fog.

The punks had followed orders and made him bleed. But they could never make him stop. Mary's imperative echoed in his head: *Harry's bar in an hour.* He stumbled onto the street, trailing blood, heedless of the pain.

Their six-month romance, story-book fantasy that it was, had finally ground to a halt. The details of their last night were etched in his mind. He sat down in their booth at Harry's feeling frustrated, his anger at the boiling point. As he had grown closer to her, falling in love in a helpless, head-over-heels kind of way, she became more distant, her life wrapped in mystery. He knew so little about her. Where did she live? Did she have a family? A job? She smiled and shook her head. They loved each other, she said. That would have to be enough. Finally, after downing his second Hurricane of the night, he blurted out, "I love you. Let me in. Otherwise this whole thing is over."

"Please don't do this, Andy." A sad smile.

He blacked out. When he woke up, Mary was gone. Her scarf lay draped across the booth. The waiter approached, looking at him strangely. Andy was embarrassed. How long had he been passed out?

"Too bad your lady didn't show," the waiter said. "You sat here drinking Hurricanes—arguing with yourself. Then, all of a sudden, you pass out."

Andy jumped to his feet, waving his arms. "She was sitting right there." He threw a fist at the waiter, slipped and fell across a booth full of diners. The manager told him to leave and not come back. Andy never knew exactly what had happened, only that Mary was gone—if she had ever really been there at all.

Her disappearance threw him into panic.

He searched the beach that night, roamed the streets until dawn. He finally called the police. After a cursory investigation they blew him off. No evidence of foul play, they said. Just another lover's quarrel.

He ended up passed out in his VW bus. For a month he spent all his time looking for her, all the while rehearsing his apology. He had always had a gift of gab, he could convince her—except that she had disappeared. Leaving him with endless, empty days. All his co-workers at the Mexican restaurant laughed at him, "*Estupido, un loco en el amor*," convinced he had made up the story of a dream lover appearing on the beach. After awhile, he began to wonder if it were true.

He took to sitting on Hendry's Beach staring at the ocean, hoping maybe somehow she would materialize again. Too many absences cost him his job. No money for rent, thrown out of his apartment. Living in his VW bus. When it got repossessed, he ended up sleeping under a bridge, tortured by his fevered dreams. A derelict who spent his days walking the streets mumbling to himself.

Now she had returned, and she wanted to see him. Joy surged in him. He almost forgot the pain in his leg as he stumbled along Las Positas. Blood on his pants leg glistened in the passing headlights. The fog was thicker now. Las Positas curved through a grove of trees and up a hill. He staggered upward, legs straining.

At the top, he bent over, hands on knees, gasping for breath. Spots of light floated before his eyes. Sweat soaked his torn sweater, his filthy cargo pants were caked with blood. He ran his fingers through his matted hair. He couldn't remember the last time he had bathed. He could smell himself. A madman from under the bridge. How could he face Mary like this? The fog pressing around him carried an aura of doom.

The wound in his leg bled freely now, blood trickling into his rotting tennis shoe. The blood loss sapped his strength. He couldn't go much farther. He retrieved a tee-shirt from his bag, fashioned a make-shift bandage.

Once, out of desperation, he had gone to the rescue mission. They put him in rehab, talked to him about religion, urged him to take responsibility for his actions. The God talk didn't take, and, after two weeks, neither did the rehab. They kicked him out. The Hurricanes he had enjoyed at Harry's were replaced by Mad Dog 20-20 in a paper bag.

The mall that cradled Harry's Bar was laid out in an "L" shape with Harry's at the corner. Andy stumbled across the parking lot toward the red "Harry's" sign.

The old woman Andy had often seen outside Harry's was still there, lying on the sidewalk wrapped in her grimy sleeping bag. She pointed her finger. "You're late, Andy."

The first words he had ever heard her speak. Another unreal situation, as impossible as the ringing of a dead phone. Only his madness could explain it. "How did you know?"

"Hurry up," the old woman said.

He pushed at Harry's front door. Stuck. He slammed his shoulder against the glass and the door burst open.

He stumbled inside, found himself facing a tableau from another era: red-flocked wallpaper nearly covered by hundreds of photos reflecting a bygone time. Movie stars, sepia-toned landscapes. The Lakers battled the Bulls on a screen above the bar. In the background, a big-band rendition of "How Long Has This Been Going On?" Only a few of the red leather booths were occupied at this late hour.

The hostess frowned at the bloodied transient. "Excuse me."

He ignored her.

She reached for a telephone. Only a few minutes before the

manager would come to throw him out.

He glanced into the kitchen where he had once worked. Harsh fluorescent light glared off stainless steel. The clatter of dishes, the clink of glasses, the hum of conversation flowed around him. It all appeared so normal.

Andy spotted the empty booth, in the back corner—their booth. He and Mary had spent hours there, laughing and talking. A photograph of Robert Mitchum still glowered down from the wall. Andy had given Mary an ultimatum there, and she had vanished.

He limped to the booth. A martini glass sat empty on the table. A paper umbrella stood upright in the glass, wooden stem impaling an olive. He had seen Mary do that a hundred times.

For some reason the little tableau effected him more than he had imagined. He teared up, wiped his nose on a dirty sleeve. Mitchum's image winked at him, as if the photograph was in on some secret. Andy's eyes lost focus. The insanity was getting worse. He stumbled against the booth. His shoulders shook. But Mary had to be here—somewhere in this world that seemed more and more unreal. Maybe this was the only world where she existed.

A waiter approached, displayed his tray with a flourish. "Burnt ends."

Mary's favorite dish.

A shock went through Andy. "Who ordered this?"

"Behind you," the waiter said.

Andy spun around. There, a faint smile on her face, stood Mary. White dress, red hair flowing around her shoulders. An apparition. Not real.

"I'm imagining this," he said.

"Sit down, Andy." She slid into the booth and touched his arm. The reality of flesh on flesh hit him like an electric shock. He grabbed her hand, oblivious to the people around them. It seemed to Andy that everyone else in the room had disappeared. Tears welled up again. "I love you. I can't lose you again."

Their eyes met. "I know," she said.

"Where were you?"

"I've been here all the time."

"What are you talking about? I looked everywhere for you."

The waiter brought a Hurricane, Harry's lethal specialty, a glass full of rum, several kinds, including the 151 stuff, topped off with a splash of fruit juice. A martini for Mary.

Andy said, "I don't know if I . . . "

She raised her glass. "Salud."

Andy picked up his drink, downed half of it. Warmth flowed through him. "Why did you come back?"

"How are you doing?"

"How do you think?" His anger flowed back. "Where the hell did you disappear to? Why did you have to dump me?"

"I had no choice."

"Are you real or are you a ghost?"

Mary said, "Could a ghost do this?" She stabbed a piece of steak, bit into it with her even white teeth, chewed and swallowed.

"The police thought I killed you," Andy said.

"Maybe you did."

"Are you telling me you're dead?"

"Not exactly."

"So what are you . . . exactly? Where did you go?"

"A place you couldn't follow."

"You're being mysterious again. I love you—loved you."

"You don't look so good."

"I know you must be disgusted with me now. Sorry, I don't even have a change of clothes. Used my last shirt for a bandage." He gestured at his bloody leg.

"That will heal," Mary said.

His vision blurred, the room spun. "Remember what you said when we met on the beach. I asked what you were doing down there. I was worried. It was late, you were alone. You said, 'I come down here now and then, when I need to.' Come down from where?"

Mary shook her head.

"But you called me," Andy said.

"And you came. That's good, because time is running out."

Something in her tone chilled him. Her smile seemed forced. Her cheekbones stood out on parched skin. Her hair had faded to a pale gray. Her shoulders looked narrower, her back hunched. It had to be a trick of the light.

"Mary." His anguished cry.

A blue glow bloomed around their booth, which nobody else in the bar seemed to notice. Cold wind rushed over them. His vision dimmed. His head spun. He braced himself against the table, fighting to stay conscious. She let go of his hand and smiled a sad smile. Her image faded. The wind grew stronger. The blast slammed the front door open, showering the floor with shards of glass. The tiny umbrella spiraled away.

The wind died, the blue light disappeared, and he was alone in the booth. Mary's scarf lay crumpled on the cushion.

He sat there in a stupor struggling to understand what had happened. His shoulders shook. Mary couldn't just disappear. Blackened bits of steak, burnt ends, lay in a congealing puddle of grease on his plate. The waiter approached.

Andy said, "Did you see. . ."

The waiter looked around, searching for the source of the voice.

Andy waved his hand. "I'm right here."

The man ignored him, picked up their plates, and walked toward the kitchen.

Andy dodged through the tables to the bar. "Did you see a woman in a white dress?" The bartender ignored him. He peeked into the kitchen, shouted her name. Again, no one paid him any attention. He dashed into the ladies room. A woman looked in the mirror, putting on lipstick. Another hiked up her skirt, adjusted her panty hose. Both women ignored him. Finally, the realization hit him. He was invisible. Just like Mary. He searched every corner of the restaurant. Nothing. He remembered the old woman by the door. She knew his name, knew he was late, knew about Mary.

He stumbled toward the front door dragging his wounded leg behind him. The background music followed him. "Moonlight in Vermont."

The parking lot lay in darkness. The old woman was gone. Her sleeping bag lay discarded by the door. A flash of movement caught his eye across the parking lot. A figure in white running away.

The manager rushed up, grabbed his arm. "Hey, man, you forgot something." He held out a slip of paper. "Fifty-one ninety." Apparently, Andy was no longer invisible.

He patted his pockets. A disingenuous pantomime. He had no money—not even a wallet. "Left my card in the car."

The manager tightened his grip on Andy's arm. "I warned you." He reached for the walkie-talkie on his belt.

"No, wait. I'll just go get—" He jerked his arm free and ran after the figure in white.

He felt the Hurricane kick in as he ran. Her image blurred, went in and out of focus. How much blood had he lost? She ran down the hill, toward the ocean. He followed, weaving along the sidewalk.

At the corner, blackness washed over him.

He woke up to the sound of the ocean, opened his eyes. Crushing headache, eyes burning, pain coursing through his body. Even in the dim light he recognized the parking lot at Hendry's Beach. A figure in white bent over him, face lost in shadow.

The woman led him along the sand to the rocky outcropping where he and Mary met. The fog drifted away, leaving the beach washed in the light of a gibbous moon. She stopped and faced him. The shock of recognition took Andy's breath away. Mary. She seemed even older now, shrunken. The rising tide swirled around her ankles, wetting the hem of her dress.

"What's happened to you?"

"What happens to all of us." She handed him a white rose.

"I don't suppose that's for me?"

She smiled. "It is now."

He reached for it, glanced down at his withered, age-spotted hands. "My god, no."

The wind picked up, driving rows of whitecaps toward the beach. The blue glow again rose around them, giving the scene an eerie, underwater cast. He took a tentative step toward her.

The water swirled around her knees. She stumbled against the thrust of it. Her twisted fingers clutched at the hem of her dress.

"Don't be afraid." She backed farther into the ocean.

"No farther, Mary. Please."

As she waded deeper, her face became a web of creases, her hands—now blackened talons—reached for him. He pulled her scarf from around his shoulders and held it out. She spread it on the water. He stared at it, mesmerized. The now familiar blue glow enveloped them. They started a slow, ritualistic dance, deeper into the ocean. Water rose to Andy's waist, his chest. He fought the panic rising in his chest, struggled to get his breath.

"I can't lose you again."

"You won't this time." Mary held out her hands, beckoning him. The water seemed warmer then. Her white hair floated a moment on the surface then disappeared. Green eyes stared up at him through the translucent water. A feeling of peace washed over him. He sank back into his mother's arms.

Only the scarf remained, undulating on the water, blue and green stripes luminescent in the light of the gibbous moon.

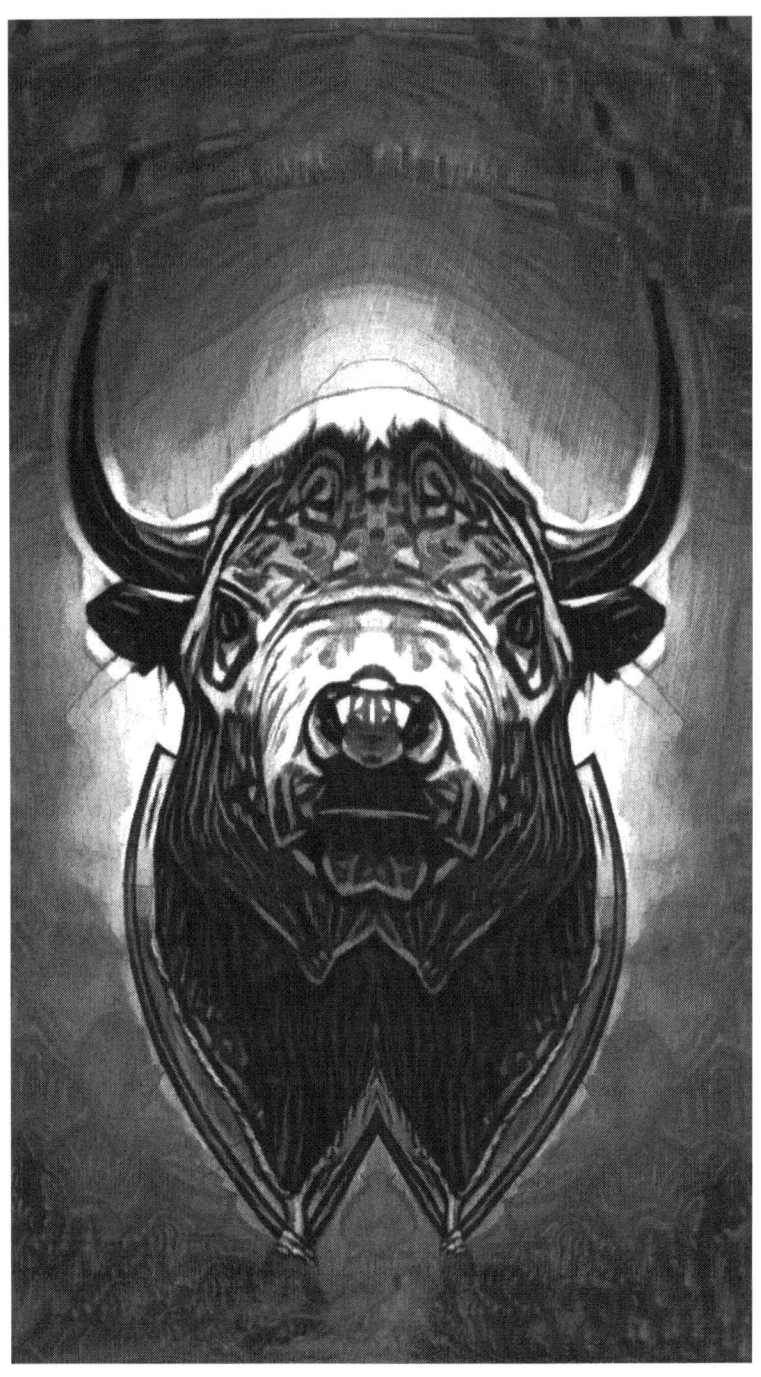
"Bull" by Grace Rachow

East Toward the Sun

by Christine Casey Logsdon

Veronica Martin slid into the circular booth near the Caballero Room, waiting. She'd grown up in Santa Barbara, long before Jerry's Bar opened in the 1960s. She had worked for the de la Guerra family, made the city thrive after the mission lands were seized, and known Thomas Hope on the broad dirt streets downtown.

Then she had met Juan, and life had changed.

Time meant little to creatures who traveled over it, and while she had once despised the events others blamed for Mexico's losses and the changes in the land, she accepted them now. Gold, greed, and oil changed the face of the city—of the world.

She had learned to appreciate her place, in time and outside it, and the way she changed so little now, while others were born and grew old and died.

She wanted a drink, and looked for a waiter. A familiar woman hustled by in a black-and-white uniform.

"Sally!" Veronica called.

Plump and fast in her fifties, Sally had blonde hair with gray roots. "You never age," she said when she stepped up to the booth. "Are you waiting for Juan?"

Veronica nodded. "Have you seen him?"

Sally shook her head. "Can I get you something while you wait?"

"Cosmopolitan. Thanks."

Sally bustled off, dropping Veronica's order at the bar. Veronica missed Juan's quiet farmhouse that had rested on this exact spot a century ago. But she loved the atmosphere here: red-and-gold damask wallpaper and wood-panel wainscoting, maroon leather and brass buttons. The deep, pillowed booths that lined the walls looked suited for movies from the 1940s, and the restaurant reeked of fried food, old wood, and good memories. It drew people from all walks, all natures, all light and shadow.

Veronica fiddled with her purse, self-conscious in a booth for six, but Juan liked these opulent, half-circle tables. In exchange for his travel services, she obliged him in any way she could.

She waited for her drink and wished Juan would get here. She'd broken something in time. The creatures who traveled time were beyond her comprehension. Like any gods, she wouldn't risk their wrath. Juan would know what to do.

She sipped her Cosmo, so strong she might have lit the vodka on fire. Jerry's appeal lay in its old-fashioned flair, good greasy appetizers, and heavy pours of decent spirits— that, and the fact that Jerry's foundations rested on some kind of soft spot in the fabric of the world.

Veronica raised her glass to toast the mounted cattle heads, silent sentinels above the door to the Caballero Room. They had hung in Juan's home, before they had come here. What stories would they tell, if they could? Tales of the creatures who appeared and disappeared from Juan's sitting room, whisked to other places and times? Now, with newer walls, guests read menus unaware, getting too drunk to drive, their excited teenagers taking control of car keys. Weddings, anniversaries, illicit affairs. Even regular patrons would glance up and gawk at the mounted cattle heads and the hundreds of photographs that covered the walls, trying to piece together a single mangled history from black and white and sepia.

Would those cattle busts share the magic tales?

Veronica frowned and sipped again at her drink. Probably they'd report how offended they'd been watching people eat steak for two hundred years.

She scooted around the booth so she could see the entrance, framed by Tiffany-styled lamps in the shape of tulips. It was the only public entrance, so Juan wouldn't enter that way. No, Juan would slip in through a kitchen freezer, or conjure himself in the men's room and step out with a flourish and she would feel her gut tighten and her knees weaken in unrequited, pointless desire. Juan had that effect on mortals, some pheromone that spanned the spaces between bodies.

"No deep-fried ravioli?"

She spilled her Cosmo. "Damn it, Juan!"

He slid into the booth beside her, shark's smile and green eyes, skin as dark and smooth as the restaurant's wood paneling.

"That's me." He took her Cosmo and sipped, made a face. "Disgusting. Waiter!" He snapped his fingers like some French aristocrat from the 1800s.

Veronica took her drink back, careful not to touch him. "Why has no one ever shot you?"

"Because I stay out of Florida," he said with a flourish of his hand.

Because he was Juan, a waiter sprinted over.

"Martini," Juan said. "Dirty, three olives, don't skimp on the gin. Off with you." He made a shooing motion.

The waiter nodded and ran.

Veronica flattened her lips, resisting a sneer. "Just back from a Pride parade?"

"What?" Juan looked down at his hand. "Too limp? Gay-adjacent? Is that what you mean?"

"You seem more flamboyant than usual."

He tugged at his shirtsleeves, his perfectly tailored suit jacket.

"Will you please turn off that sparkle?" Veronia said.

"No." He grinned.

His drink arrived, and Veronica ordered deep-fried ravioli before the waiter disappeared.

"Thank you for coming," she said.

Juan shrugged. "I saw your ad, had nothing else to do. It's been a while."

"I need your help, Juan. Another Jerry's, before 1997."

"Why 'when'? I've never known you to care about the 'when'."

Sally arrived with the ravioli; she must have stolen someone else's order. "Here you are, Juan." Her cheeks were flushed.

Juan rubbed his hands together. "Right here. All of it, right here. Veronica has no taste, she hates these things."

Sally didn't even look at Veronica. "Can I get you anything else, Juan? A drink? Anything at all?"

"I'm good for now, thanks." Juan ignored her and dug in. "Oh, my bits of stuffed, doughy heaven."

Veronica tightened her resolve against her desire for him. Like a desire to know God, it would never be satisfied or understood, so she grit her teeth and examined photographs on the wall behind his head.

Juan dipped a ravioli in sauce. "Why 1997?"

"Something happened."

He chewed and swallowed. "A lot of things happened. Mars landing and Hale-Bopp. Chad's independence and Hong Kong's repossession. Sheep cloning and an incredibly rude reference to Dolly Parton's breasts, if you want my opinion."

She shook her head. "No, I mean—something didn't happen. Can't you see the change, Juan?"

He blinked, fork frozen over another ravioli. "Change? Nothing changes."

"So you've said. But I traveled not long ago. When I returned to Jerry's, Princess Diana was alive. Is alive, now. Today, in 2019. And England has a king. Your kind has always said that time was immutable, a structure like this building. But things are different."

Juan closed his eyes and she watched his lips move, his brows drawn together in concentration. His head jerked up and he scanned the room—for what, Veronica couldn't guess.

"Mother Teresa," he said. "Dios mios, Agnes. Father Bergoglio..." His eyes pierced her with accusation. "How did a gringa like you change the course of the Catholic church?"

"Can you fix it?" Veronica's fingers itched for a rosary she no longer carried: a talisman against this being and all he represented.

"I don't know what to fix, or how."

Her head began to swirl from too much vodka. The room began to spin. She pressed her palms flat against the cold glass that covered the tablecloth. "Something's wrong. Juan, I..." She reached for his hand, and when she touched his skin, fire shot up her fingers.

He clutched her before she could pull away. "Warn a man next time."

Veronica felt a different pain chase up her abused nerves, calming the burn in her arm but not the rest of her. "You're m-making it worse."

Juan frowned. "Something's wrong."

"I s-s-said t-that."

He stood, grabbed Veronica around the ribs, and cut a path across the room. "Don't show your face," he said. Her body felt rag-doll limp, held together by knocking bones whose knots were loose. She was coming apart at the core. "What's... wh—"

"Someone is trying to tear apart your soul."

"N-not the drink?" Her arm flopped forward as he walked. What spectacle must they be making? But there was no pregnant silence, no shocked stillness around them, just the clank of cutlery and glasses and ice, and the noise of voices and music and people.

Her knees buckled. Her head lolled forward, chin to chest. The zipper of her sweater cut into the skin of her neck. "I c—c..."

"Sorry. Sorry," he said, soothing where he'd been harsh before. "Someone in the pictures, I can't find them. We have to go."

Juan strode with her into the ladies' room and pushed her into an open stall.

"It's time," he said.

Finally, she felt a familiar twist inside her cells that said nature was shifting, and God blinked.

The terrible ripping sensation was gone.

They stood in the salon of an old Spanish ranch house. Bright afternoon sun spilled through windows that opened from the central courtyard.

She pushed herself away from Juan's supporting arm. "What happened?"

"I told you," he said. "Your soul was being torn apart." He went to a side table and handed her a glass of water.

She felt the weight of the crystal glass, the deeply etched designs sharp against her skin. She gulped the water. Her hand shook.

Juan rounded on her, and she felt nothing of her usual attraction. But she did feel the fear.

"1997. Why do you want to go to 1997?"

She looked around the room to avoid looking at him. There were no lamps, no computers, no cameras or wireless routers. "When are we?"

"1851, and we're staying here until you tell me what you did." He stared at her and waited. A clock ticked, loud from some other room. She heard the occasional cluck of a chicken, but other than that—nothing. Just Juan's breaths.

"My face hasn't aged in a long time. Staying in one place is uncomfortable, so I went backward to Los Angeles, for years. When they re-opened the Harvey Room at Union Station, I took a job as a server and waited until someone like you arrived. They returned me to Jerry's in my time, my home, but some things were wrong, like I said."

He huffed. "Five royal offspring of Diana. No Brexit. A different pope. No Saint Teresa. No Syrian war."

Veronica stuck her hands into the pockets of her jeans, felt the foreboding chill of time. She hadn't known so many things were wrong.

"What did you do in Los Angeles?"

"I was a costume designer in Hollywood. I used a lot of cocaine. I wasn't conspicuous."

He snapped his fingers. "More."

"Plastic," she said. "American Express cards. Gold."

He made a reaching motion with his hand. "Another."

"The AOL CDs that were everywhere. People used them as coasters. Made clothes and art from them."

"More."

"The sound of a dial-up computer. Horses on studio lots, the sound of iron shoes on concrete."

He beckoned with his fingers, demanding more, so she gave it.

"Cocaine. Common as cigarettes in my circles. Some hotels, a housekeeper couldn't clean a coffee table without first wiping the powder away. The Internet. CNN. News coming faster. Flashbulbs. Tabloid magazines in supermarkets. Paparazzi."

He snapped his fingers and pointed at her. "Let's find suitable clothes. It's time to travel."

In the hallway, they passed the family's altar, tucked in an alcove, and Veronica stopped.

A small bowl beneath the Lady of Guadalupe held rosaries with beads of rough-polished robles wood threaded on twine.

"You should take one," Juan said. "A saint is no longer a saint, and a Jesuit isn't the bishop of Rome."

She dropped the rosary around her neck, crossed herself again, and turned up the hall.

"I'm sorry," he said as he took the lead.

"For what?" They climbed stairs, and she watched his body stride through hard slashes of sun and shadow, all but disappearing between the bright beams.

He entered a bedroom and turned to look at her. "Everything bad that has happened and will happen to you." He surveyed her clothes. "Your shoes are fine, but the rest must go. You look like a man."

She touched the crude crucifix under her shirt, went to the wardrobe, and selected a dress she might have worn in her youth, cream-colored with neat embroidery and a wide leather belt. When she was done, Juan held out his hand.

She took it, and again God blinked.

They stood in a stone building. She looked out a window onto an early industrial town, its high-pitched roofs dark with soot. Chimneys in factories not far away choked coal smoke into the air, and early automobiles with spoked wheels and high suspensions weaved around wagons and pedestrians.

"Are we in Europe?"

"Yes. Üsküp, 1924." He waved away her questions. "Not important. We won't be here long."

They walked down a hallway and into a dressing room. He grabbed a cloak from a hook and tossed it to her.

When they opened the side door and stepped into an alley, the smell of rotting meat and human waste hit her nose. She gagged, hand on her belly.

"Start walking," he said. "It'll help."

She watched Juan's heels a few feet in front of her. Morning mist rose from damp ground. Her head swam and the fear of fainting kept her silent.

"It's just up here," Juan said after half a mile or so.

"What is?"

"Agnes's home."

"Agnes?"

"Anjezë Gonxe Bojaxhiu." Juan frowned back at her. "Mother Teresa. You didn't know her name?"

"I..." she felt her mouth open and close. "I never thought I'd meet a saint."

"She's not a saint here. She's fourteen."

"What does she know, at fourteen, that will help you?"

"She knew the day she would die. If it's still the 5th of September in 1997, we have one kind of problem. If it's not, we have another kind of problem."

"I was only in L.A. for a decade, Juan. I don't think—"

"Let me do the thinking, my friend." Juan lifted a brass knocker affixed to a heavy wood door.

A tiny, ancient woman opened it.

"My dear," Juan said, as if he spoke to the child she might have been once, then he switched to a foreign tongue. The old woman led them into the house.

Veronica recognized enough words to get "Juan" and

"urgent" and "Agnes."

The old woman offered food and drink, made him as welcome as a relative. She pulled an *ibrik* from her stove and poured thick Turkish coffee into earthenware cups. Veronica sipped the black sweet coffee while Juan and the woman talked.

After a couple of minutes, the woman refilled their cups and left them alone.

Juan shifted to English. "Agnes is at her morning prayers in the nearby convent. She didn't become a saint through lack of faith or fortitude." He waved a hand. "After prayers, she'll return here. We're welcome to make ourselves at home until she arrives."

"Is it ever boring," Veronica asked, "having people just hand everything to you?"

Juan's eyebrows rose in surprise. "There are planes where I'm barely tolerated. Places I'm not even allowed without proper disguise."

"Huh."

He grinned. "Can't imagine it, can you? Well, you'll have decades to think about it."

Half an hour later, jittering from Turkish coffee and sugar, Veronica jumped when the door hinges squeaked and a diminutive teen walked into the house carrying her Bible and rosary. Familiar eyes in a line-less face, the fire of devotion shining in them, the wizened woman she would become already lived inside her. She nodded politely to them both, merely curious—unmoved by what Juan was.

All of them Catholics, Latin was their common language. No, Teresa had not dreamed the time of her death. She knew nothing of Juan or Veronica or any changes in her future.

But, she said, the future wasn't written, and dreams were only dreams.

Juan nodded. "Thank you, miss. We'll be on our way." He took Veronica's hand, and when they stepped through the front door of the young woman's house, God blinked.

Teresa's door took them from Macedonia to Kolkata, from the young woman's house of prayer to a thriving convent, to a different and more modern stench. Motorbikes and tuk-tuks crowded the roads, and an open-sided truck exiting the convent carried a group of nuns in blue-trimmed saris.

"We're in a hurry. I know a way in," Juan said.

"We're sneaking into a nunnery?"

He scowled. "To see the wrong mother."

Veronica touched her cross and ducked her head. She missed Santa Barbara, wanted the comfort of familiarity. She wanted the world set right.

In minutes, Juan had skirted gaggles of roving women and gained entrance to a private room befitting a sultan.

Mother Teresa stood with two feminine creatures so magnetic, they must be of Juan's kind. The nun's face looked different: angrier, harder. The beings beside her seemed aloof at best.

"I..." she swallowed, looked to Juan for guidance, but his face was so flushed she could see the dark spots of blood under his skin. He looked anywhere but at any of them.

"I'm so sorry," Veronica said to the Mother. "I don't know what happened. I don't remember anything odd—"

"Paparazzi," Mother Teresa said. "The paparazzi."

"What?"

She stomped her foot. "You were in Los Angeles. Paparazzi thrive there. Paparazzi chased Diana to her death. Without her death, there was nothing and no one to shroud my own. That is the intersection of what was and what was not."

Veronica blinked, but her mind made little sense of the words. "I... how can you know?"

"How can you not!" For a tiny woman, she had the force of ages behind her voice. "Go! And you," she said, shifting her focus to Juan. "Stop the motion of the danger. This child altered ascensions of the church that would fix what others have broken."

He nodded. "Understood."

When God blinked, they were back in the bathroom at Jerry's.

Juan stood at the sink, washing his hands and staring at himself in the mirror. "Our booth should be empty," he said. "Would you order ravioli? I'll be right out."

Veronica nodded. She'd never moved so quickly through so many rooms of time. She felt sick, dizzy, still afraid.

Outside the bathroom, fewer patrons filled the room.

Their booth was empty, set for five. Sally was working. She looked for Juan when Veronica sat down. "Hi, honey. Need anything? For you, or for two?"

"Water, please," she said, and swiped sweat off her forehead. "And deep-fried ravioli for Juan."

Juan joined her after a moment, sliding into the booth across the table. He looked around. "Did you order?"

"Yes. This is almost the night we left, isn't it? Is everything all right, now?"

"You did something. I don't know, maybe you overdosed a photographer. Maybe you used his cocaine and he went straight. You did—probably one very small thing that can't be done. Then that man did or didn't do one very important thing. Then a mass of photographers didn't chase Princess Diana to her death on August 31. Then after that, without Diana's death to distract the world, Mother Teresa's death was an international day of mourning, and the ensuing media frenzy into her life created an impediment to her canonization. Then something else changed because of you, and something else, and something else, until Agnes before she was Teresa didn't dream. And Cardinal Bergoglio did not become Pope Francis, and the Catholic Church turned in a ruinous direction."

Juan's eyes still scanned the room, resting for a second on a table of patrons, for another on a photograph, and for another still on the halo refractions around the lamps.

"I didn't know you could impact things the way you did. The Mother told me to stop the motion of the danger. You'll need to stay here for a while."

The words shouldn't frighten her. "Of course. This is my home."

His face, rarely sorrowful, took on the grief of a Christ painting.

"I'm glad you like it here." He blinked and his green eyes glazed with tears. He was at once alluring and terrible, and she remembered that among the angels, Lucifer had been the most beautiful.

He moved before she could think. He was fast. She'd always known. Forks and an empty appetizer plate skittered off the table and onto the carpeted floor, a muted thud of ceramic that no one heard. His hands held her wrists, pushing them into the booth's heavy leather padding, and his chest pressed against her face, not-quite smothering.

"It won't be long," he said.

She felt cocooned, swaddled, flattened like when they slipped between times and places.

"A hundred years," he said. "Maybe a little more."

New panic washed through her. A hundred years was almost all of the life she'd lived so far. A hundred years of what? Her heart should be pounding, but she couldn't feel its beat anymore.

"I'll do everything I can to let you out."

She wished he hadn't said that. Already, she was looking down on him, and she couldn't see herself in the booth. Juan settled in like he'd been alone all along. No one looked his way.

A diner laughed, and the sound cut at her: for a moment everyone in the room, perhaps in all of time and space, had been silent and frozen.

Juan looked up at the wall—at her—and tears spilled over, bright streaks on his dark cheeks. She was hanging there, flat and framed. She knew this picture: women dancing, the familiar-seeming girl in the center with big eyes and dark lips smiling out at the room. How many pictures had she hung in? How many more to come?

Across the room she could see thousands of other people in hundreds of other photographs, all of them looking back. The photographs, some as old as she was and some the bright colors of this century, they all lived past the static images in their frames.

She could see the cattle heads, mounted sentinels above the Caballero Room entrance. She'd imagined them alive more than once, imagined magic and untold stories inside these rooms. But it hadn't been her imagination. Their eyes watched her. Their stiff necks would have swiveled. They would have nodded, if they could.

"*El Rancho* Steel" by Violet Sayre

Closing Credits

by Dennis Russell

"Under blue *El Rancho* skies
The morning air is fine
We'll head out on that trail
Friend by friend, side by side

New adventures we will find
Open pastures we will ride
where the streams and rivers wind
under blue *El Rancho* skies"

—First Verse of "Blue *El Rancho* Skies," opening theme from *El Rancho* film and television series

Carlos Garcia pulled open the door of Gary's Steakhouse and Grill and stepped inside. He took off his sunglasses and put them in his jacket pocket, and paused for a moment to let his eyes adjust to the dim barroom light. He grimaced and waved off the hostess at the front desk and took a quick scan around the front dining room and bar. Every booth and barstool was red diamond-tufted Naugahyde, and the floor was covered in green short-pile carpet. "Gary's" was spelled in blue stained glass in the lamps above every table. Carlos flashed a smile and waved hello to Darla, who had been working at Gary's since the place was established in 1959.

She must be the oldest waitress in any diner in any town, Carlos thought. Darla didn't wave back. She never waved back. He quickly walked through the archway to the second, larger dining room, decorated with historic photographs of the city of St. Hervé and some of its famous residents, and kept on to his final destination. He pushed open the stained-glass doors of El Rancho Sky Room and shut the door that separated the monthly meeting of *Los Hermanos Benéficos* from the regular patrons of the restaurant.

Most patrons of Gary's never saw the inside of El Rancho Sky Room, but it was a quite familiar place to Carlos. To his left was the restroom for the exclusive use of El Rancho Sky Room patrons. The next third of the wall was lined with La Cantina, the oak bar that served the banquet room guests. For *Los Hermanos Benéficos* meetings, the top-shelf liquor was moved to the bottom shelf, as most of the members displayed their financial status through upscale alcohol. Carlos winked and shot his index finger gun-like at the bartender and went straight to the end of the bar, where five chafing dishes held today's *Benéfico* buffet. One dish was filled with cheese enchiladas (for the vegetarians), another dish was filled with buffalo chicken wings, the third held slices of tri-tip, the fourth held miniature versions of Gary's "world renowned" ham and cheese sandwiches, and the fifth contained Gary's "famous" Hot Tots potatoes (tater tots with bacon and jalapenos). Neither of the world famous dishes were really very well known outside the doors of Gary's.

There are varying degrees of fame, Carlos thought, as he used the stainless steel tongs to transfer some of the famous wings and Hot Tots onto his tiny plate. A few feet past the end of the bar was a round table where Carlos grabbed a slice of sourdough bread, a pat of butter, and a small paper ramekin with Gary's special salsa. For those, like Carlos, who didn't imbibe expensive liquor, there were glasses of water and iced tea. For the sloppy, there were extra napkins. Carlos grabbed a few.

Buffalo wings are pretty sloppy eating, thought Carlos. Before stepping away from the table, he reached down and took a few more. The drunken members of *Los Hermanos Benéficos* were always bumping into somebody, and with the tiny plates and strong drinks, there was a good chance of getting sauce on your shirt.

Besides the restroom, the bar, the round bread table, the carefully arranged dining tables with red and white tablecloths, and chairs to seat *Los Hermanos Benéficos,* the rest of the décor was a shrine to *Los Hermanos Benéficos* founder, Cal Evans. Everyone in the world knew the first verse of the theme song to the western series *El Rancho.* Between the years of 1952 and 1959, Cal Evans' voice yodeled it over the opening credits of 125

Sunday night television episodes and five feature films. Cal was the last and the biggest of the Singin' Cowboys. He was a true icon: a nostalgic symbol of the American West, representing the mythological chivalrous code of the courageous, courteous cowpoke.

A glass shadowbox displayed a pair of fringed tan leather gloves that Cal wore in one season of the TV show, alongside a pearl-handled Colt 45 revolver in a tooled leather holster, a Cal Evans lunchbox, a deck of Cal Evans playing cards, and three different Cal Evans collector badges that had only been available in select boxes of *El Rancho* Rings breakfast cereal. Next to the case was a beautifully seasoned brown leather saddle, the actual one that Cal swung on to the back of his horse Mercury at the beginning of every ride. Intricate hand-tooled roses and vines offset silver and turquoise inlay.

Carlos had been a huge fan of Cal Evans and *El Rancho* when he was a kid. He and his father watched reruns every Saturday morning. He thought it was worth donating his time to be the accountant for *Los Hermanos Benéficos* just to be able to marvel at the saddle once a month. Even better, hovering like a halo above the saddle and the case was one of Cal's grey felt ten-gallon cowboy hats, with a beaded band that also contained a fair amount of turquoise and silver. Carlos glanced over to a modest corner that displayed the poncho, sombrero, and fake oversized moustache of Cal's comedic sidekick, Pedro "Pappy" Sanchez.

The other walls of El Rancho Sky Room were lined with enormous photographs, mostly group photos, taken during the yearly *Los Hermanos Benéficos* charity horse rides and parades.

Cal Evans and Pappy Sanchez were central figures in most of them. Carlos had never been on one of the rides. He was more of a desk jockey than any kind of *vaquero*. Looking at the photos, though, he could imagine the ride: the smells of leather, horse shit, beer, whiskey, and barbeque.

Carlos stood, studying the photographs one-by-one while eating his wings and tots. By looking at them sequentially, he felt he was looking at a time lapse photo of these men's lives. A single moment stood out to Carlos, blown up, poster-sized, glass-covered, and wood-framed. A small plaque below that particular picture bore the etched words "Music on the Trail." Though he had seen it many times, today for some reason, this photo particularly intrigued him. It made him think of the bridge to the song "Blue *El Rancho* Skies."

> "Out on the breeze, there's a pretty melody
> If you hear it, come on, sing along
> We've got no cares, just some stories to share
> And a place where we all belong."

Carlos looked deeper and deeper into the photograph, trying to join with the black-and-white images behind the glass. There were several men in it. Cal was there with his guitar, singing. An unknown, hatless cowboy plucked a banjo. A plate of fried chicken and a few beer bottles sat on a barrel head. Carlos settled his eyes on a man in the foreground, in profile, squeezing an accordion. Carlos studied the face of "Pappy" Sanchez. He mimicked the beaming smile Cal's co-star always had when he was playing accordion and singing.

Carlos shuffled closer to the glass of the photo, his own face superimposed its reflection on the glass. It was as if he was there among them. Carlos also saw in the reflection the one remaining buffalo wing on his plate; it looked as if was stacked with the fried chicken in the photo. Feeling like a cowboy on the trail, he heartily took an enormous bite out of it.

Just at that moment, Justin Clay passed by on his way from the restroom back to his seat. He slapped Carlos's back and said "You hear music out of that, dude? Isn't that the best kind of accordion? The silent kind?" Justin laughed at his own joke all the way to back to the table where all the car-dealing *Los Hermanos Benéficos* sat.

With Justin's slap, the bite of buffalo wing shifted from Carlos's mouth to the back of his throat and wedged there. He tried a quick cough to dislodge it, but no luck. The sauce was dripping into his trachea and started to burn. He gave a couple of coughs with no better luck. He hurried to grab a glass of water from the banquet table. He downed it. Still stuck. He downed another. Still no luck and the water caused more sauce to dilute and drip further down his windpipe, causing it to burn even more. He grabbed a napkin and coughed into it. Nothing came up.

Carlos knew he'd need to cough stronger and louder to get the meat cleared. He didn't want to make any kind of scene. He ran to the exclusive El Rancho Sky Room restroom.

Thank God, thought Carlos. The restroom was unoccupied.

He stumbled in and locked the door. He put his hands on his knees and heaved several loud coughs. Still, the wing stuck like a cork in a champagne bottle. He thrusted his abdomen against the sink, trying a self-Heimlich maneuver, but it didn't work. Again, again, and again he rammed his stomach against the sink. He began to sweat. His face was turning white. His lips were turning blue.

On the other side of the bathroom door, Carlos heard Dylan Johnson's voice. "C'mon, you gonna take all day?" Dylan knocked on the door. At first politely, then more aggressively. "I gotta piss!"

Dammit, I'm gonna die like Mama Cass Elliot, choking on a goddam chicken wing. Or was it a fucking ham sandwich? thought Carlos. *On the other hand, I'll be like Elvis, the King. I'll be found on the floor next to the toilet. Except it won't be my own toilet!*

Carlos tried to yell to Dylan for help, but with no air behind them, the words wouldn't come out. He wanted to unlock the door, but his hands still gripped the sides of the sink and, without any oxygen to power them, none of his other muscles moved either.

He heard Dylan pound harder and more incessantly. "Hey, man, hurry up! C'mon? Are you dying in there?" Dylan pounded a couple of more times, and then no more. Carlos heard Dylan's footsteps pad away quickly over the green carpet and then the swing of the stained glass door. He stared into the mirror and fell forward. His forehead rested on the mirror. No breath fogged the glass. He thought he saw, mixed with his reflection, the profile of Pappy Sanchez playing the accordion and Cal Evans holding a guitar with his mouth open in song. The periphery of Carlos's vision turned to black, and the black closed in to a pinpoint sunset dot of light in the mirror. All

Carlos could see before him was a deep, dark, empty black screen.

Carlos slumped to the floor, his fingers relaxing their grasp on the porcelain sink. His head thumped against the plastic toilet paper dispenser before tumbling down to meet the cool, hard tile. In the black, he saw a white light come into view, at first undistinguishable, but quickly finding focus. The names of the most important people in Carlos's life rolled up the black screen.

>Carlos Miguel Garcia, Jr. as The Father
>Sandra Jessica Trask as The Mother
>Jessica Jennifer Garcia as The Sister
>David Jesus Garcia as The Brother
>Carlos Miguel Garcia as The Grandfather
>Maria Consuela Lopez as The Grandmother
>Patrick "Cal" Evans as The Good Guy
>Pedro "Pappy" Sanchez as The Sidekick

Those were the only names he could make out. Subsequent names rolled faster and faster until Carlos couldn't keep up with them. The list spun into a white blur down the center of the black screen, a consciousness of closing credits. Orchestra music swelled, then fell in decrescendo. In waltz time, a simple strummed guitar accompanied two voices and accordion. It was the closing theme of *El Rancho*, the final verse to "Blue *El Rancho* Skies."

"Though we've wandered far and wide

When we come to end our ride
We'll pleasantly abide
Un-der Bluuuuueeeeee
    El Raaaaan-chooooo
        Skiiiiiiieeeeees."

"Woman, Spectral" by Violet Sayre

The Hurricane: Mercury in Retrograde

by Silver Webb

Jenny Mandisi walks in a web of light. Spider-fine threads of sensation travel from her, over the parking lot of Loreto Plaza. Above the faux Spanish architecture of stores and restaurants, the palm trees turn to tarantulas in the dusk. Jenny maneuvers around people by estimation of threat, intention, potential pain.

A bald man glances up from an outdoor book table, staring at Jenny's licorice black hair and dress, her spectral face.

"Is that your Halloween costume, honey?"

Jenny is not twelve years old, and this is not her Halloween costume. She is forty. In her Demonia platform Mary-Janes, she crests six foot four, her frame so spindly that she looks like a Gothic pipe cleaner.

A gust of wind whips the pages on the table, startling the man. Jenny slips past him, hurrying to the nondescript glass front of Cherry's Grill, opening the door, and pausing to let her eyes adjust. Framed photos of celebrities hang in uneasy angles on the gold wallpaper. Deep booths of quilted red leather, wagon-wheel chairs, glass lamps. To the left is the mirrored bar, to the back is a moose head on the wall. No moose ever looked so happy to be beheaded, stuffed, and nailed to a wall, overseeing the kitchen doors swinging open and shut beneath his muzzle.

A cadaverous waitress, pinched stomach like a hermit crab, motions for her to follow. Jenny sinks down into Booth #2. From here she can see the whole room.

Jenny casts her lay lines, visible only to her, latching onto the walls, people, the moose. She takes the room in this way. The awkward blind date, an old cowboy looking lonesome in the Gold Room, writers hunched together like ghostly saboteurs at the bar. She judges their distance from her, their capacities, searches for any tremor of instability, and decides the room is as safe as any place can be. She takes off her black messenger bag and puts her phone on the table.

`Sorry, late for dins.` Rolando's text appears.

`When are you not late?` Jenny types.

The waitress comes back with bread, and Jenny realizes she hasn't eaten since breakfast. White bread smeared with butter, salsa fresca, and sour cream. Jenny takes a deep bite, smudging her black lipstick, the tomato juice dripping from the corner of her mouth. When she is short of money, sometimes the bread *is* dinner.

```
There yet? Vanessa texts.
Yes, Jenny replies.
You know the rules. No alcohol.
I'm a grown woman.
If I find you with a cocktail, I will
karate-chop you.
```

Jenny has no intention of obeying her cousin. When the waitress comes by, she orders a Hurricane, the booziest drink in a bar already famed for its slutty pours.

Jenny has another bite of bread and stares at the last text Phil Fleischman sent her:

```
Great manuscript. The rewrite really
works. I'd like to talk to you about
printing this.
```

Jenny feels like she might sail out of her seat, a black-widow balloon filled with the helium of praise. After 114 rejections, she finally has a yes. For her book. *The* book. The one she's been working on for years, a manic devotion that serves as friend, lover, and reason for existing. After her nightly shift at the Granada Theater, she threads through midnight streets, the ideas come to her, spinning, spinning. An hour on foot to her rented room in San Roque, and then hours of shadow-dreams dance across her computer screen. She writes a world in which she makes sense, the only place that she does. Except perhaps Cherry's Grill, where tall tales are as common as framed photos of Ronald Reagan.

A feeling like warm honey runs down her spine, pooling in her sacrum. That means Alex is about to text her. She waits, and a second later, a message from him springs up on her screen.

`What about artichokes?` She hears the text spoken in his voice, a deep resin that rolls over her, like amber trapping a mosquito.

`Artichokes?` Jenny's thumbs fly over her phone. `Death thistles. Prickly, medieval, a rueful food that hides its elusive heart.` And for a second Jenny thinks this describes her as well. She presses send.

`So that's a no on artichokes?` The question is rhetorical. Alex doesn't eat vegetables. This is a polite exchange of formalities before they decide which end of the cow to eat. `Order me the burnt ends. Thirty minutes out.`

Jenny's heart sinks a little. If Alex and Rolando are both late, that means more time alone with—someone trips her lay lines, a presence behind her, sharp as the snap of a match—her cousin.

Vanessa Mandisi plops down across from Jenny, wearing a white suit and a Tiffany necklace, her ginger hair curled tight like fusilli pasta.

"Rolls is late. Alex too," Jenny says.

"I heard. Drunk driver on 154. Alex had to rappel down the side of a cliff. Whole family of five is toast."

Jenny blanches. Alex didn't mention a cliff. But then, Alex rarely tells her anything.

"Do we have to eat here every week?" Vanessa picks up a menu. "Is free bread that sexy?"

"We can't all be lawyers."

"District Attorney. And if I'm footing the bill, I want to pick the restaurant."

"Fine. We can go to Vegan Green. See if Alex will eat Satan tacos."

"Seitan. Sayyy-tawn. Like I care what Alex thinks, *Jennifer*."

It's not a good day if Vanessa is calling her Jennifer. On a good day, Jenny is Jewels, Vanessa is Vans, Rolando is Rolls, and Alex is still Alex because he won't answer to anything else.

Jenny sees a flicker on her phone, and her adrenaline starts to shimmer. It's a text from Phil Fleischman:

`Do you have time to talk about the book? I'd really like to move on it.`

`Sure,` she types.

`Great. King's Road?`

King's Road is a pub that gets a little rowdy at night. It's already 7. Maybe he means tomorrow.

`I like King's Road.` She's not sure what else to say.

`Great. Tonight, 11 o'clock.`

Jenny blinks. There isn't even a question mark after that 11 o'clock.

"What is it?" Vanessa asks.

"The guy from Chapala Press."

"The wiener?"

"Phil Fleischman. Why would you call him a wiener?"

"I see him at the courthouse a lot. Owes alimony all over town."

"I didn't know he was married."

Vanessa's eyes narrow. "What does he want with you?"

"He's considering my book for publication."

"He's considering your ass for penetration, and that's all."

"Your mind is a morass of ugliness."

"So why do you look like someone just stuck a machete in your black heart?"

"He wants to meet at King's Road." Jenny's face colors, although under her zombie-white foundation, it may be hard to tell. "At eleven. Tonight."

"Eleven, King's Road. Sure. Totally normal business stuff. Carry on."

"I'm not his type. I can't be. He drives a Lexus. And wears Italian leather shoes."

"Maybe he collects oddities. Bored, rich guys are like that."

Jenny sees her book in print, a world split open in the hands of others, her life somehow less lonely for it. How badly does she need that? Maybe Phil Fleischman is a nice guy.

"He isn't," Vanessa says, picking Jenny's thoughts from the air.

"You don't know that."

"I do know it. And I will shit my kidneys out my asshole if I eat any of this." Vanessa slaps the menu down.

"Have a drink then." Jenny's mouth curves. "That's gluten-free. Probably."

"Celiacs is not a joke. Don't start with me. If you think this guy just wants to talk about literature, you are hell and gone from Cartagena, Angel."

Jenny almost smiles. It's a good line. From *Romancing the Stone*. One of Vanessa's few redeeming qualities is her quotes.

"I'll show up," Vanessa says.

"Are you Patrick Swayze in *Roadhouse*? No, don't come. I can handle myself."

"My god." A deep crease appears in Vanessa's forehead. "Is this another PigSwine McDickFace? You don't like this guy, do you?"

There is a downside to cousins. They know all the dirt. Vanessa has a good memory and therefore good reason to worry. Jenny falls in love silently, glows so violently that she ignites, burns herself to ashes with the pain of the unrequited, and then crawls away, her light dimmed for years after. But she knows who she loves, and it isn't Phil Fleischman.

"I look up to Phil, that's all. He publishes good books, and he teaches great courses."

"Where, city college?"

"Quit talking at me."

Fine, Vanessa changes tactics and thinks at her. *It's taken years for you to get your life back together. Don't blow it now on some poser who's stringing you along.*

Quit thinking at me. Jenny clicks her black nails on the glass tabletop.

Fine. Vanessa gives up.

Jenny checks her phone.

A text from Rolando says, `Bus is late. Almost there.`

A text from Alex says, `Vanessa cheesing you off yet?`

`Massive cheese,` Jenny types. `Camembert. Gorgonzola.`

`There in ten. Order milk.`

Now Jenny feels bad she ordered the Hurricane. She usually listens to Alex. Even if he doesn't understand the terms of light and dark that define her world, the way she lifts and tilts and can't find her feet, the way she falls. Still, she listens to him.

`I ordered a Hurricane,` she types.

`DO. NOT. DRINK. IT,` Alex replies.

"You ordered a Hurricane?" Vanessa frowns, eavesdropping on Jenny's thoughts. "No. Absolutely not! I'm still paying Joe's Place back for what you did."

"That was your fault, not mine."

They stare at each other, eyes meeting mid-table in seige. Jenny's fingers curl a little, and the napkin by Vanessa begins to lift upward.

"Really?" Vanessa raises an eyebrow, and the candle flares. "In public?"

Jenny relents and the napkin stills. Something about Cherry's Grill makes her forget the rules of the mundane world, the imperative to feign normalcy.

Jenny's lay lines jingle. Rolando walks up behind her.

"Hay girlzs." Rolando is wearing white jeans and carrying a Hello Kitty! clutch on his wrist. He sits with the delicacy of Lady Bird, like he is cradling a bon-bon between his butt cheeks and is afraid to crush it.

"You look like death, Jewels. Something wrong?" Rolando's lips glitter at her. "Wait, you always look like death!"

"It's that guy," Vanessa says. "The wiener."

"Wieners aren't so bad, Vans. Maybe you should try one,"

Rolando says.

"I'm vegan. And this is guy is a poser. He teaches adult ed, okay?"

Jenny fumes silently, and the edges of Vanessa's hair lift and move like snakes.

Vanessa cocks her head at Jenny. "Leave my hair alone or I will rearrange your doll collection."

"Soooo," Rolando says brightly. "What's the problem?"

"He wants Jenny to meet him at King's Road. At eleven o'clock."

"Booty call, Jewels, yaz!"

Jenny's face heats. She doesn't believe in booty calls. She thinks holding hands is a big deal, like a K-O big deal.

"You want this guy to help you, better give him some sugar," Rolando says.

Jenny imagines trying to take her clothes off in front of Phil Fleischman, trying to act normal, like she isn't scared. The edges of her inner landscape darken, time closes in on her, a muddying of what was and what is.

"You're supposed to be the empath." Vanessa flicks Rolando on the shoulder. "Stop with the shit that upsets her."

"You're getting a parking ticket." Rolando smiles.

Vanessa flames her eyes at him. "I don't feel that."

"You parked in a handicapped zone, right? But you don't got no handicap sticker. There's a meter bitch out there clocking you."

Vanessa springs up and sprints out the door. Rolando unclicks his purse, takes out his tarot deck, and spreads the cards into a fan on the table.

Jenny shakes her head. "I don't want to."

"Pick a card for this guy." Rolando slides the deck closer to her.

"I'll pick the devil. Or death. I always pick death," she says.

"Tarot don't lie." Rolando shrugs.

Jenny sees the card she's supposed to pick. Of course she does. It has the resonance of blue dust hovering above it. Phil Fleischman. She flips it.

Rolando's upper lip curls. "You got the worst luck, girl."

It's the death card, a skeleton cackling and pointing at her.

"Damn it, Rolls."

"It's not, like, literal. No one is gonna die…probably." Rolando pulls Jenny's phone toward him. "What did this *chalupa* say anyways?"

She is distracted by the waitress coming to the table. But then she sees that Rolando is typing something on her phone.

"Rolls, no," Jenny hisses.

"Here's your drink." The waitress sets down a massive curved Hurricane glass, glowing pink, topped with a speared cherry.

"What are you typing?" Jenny kicks at him under the table.

"You're not no 7-11, so we're gonna tell him that." Rolando clears his throat and reads what he's typed: "Do I look like a banjee ratchet ho?"

"No, no, oh my god, no, Rolls, don't you fucking send that!"

Rolando's grin dissolves as he catches sight of the Hurricane. "Alex told you not to have no alcohol, right?"

Jenny lunges for her phone and then hears it. The whoosh sound that a text has been sent.

`Do I look like a banjee ratchet ho?` Sent. To Phil Fleischman, head of Chapala Press.

Jenny's lungs tighten. A second, ten seconds, a minute, two. There is no reply. Nothing. He is not going to text back. Jenny shoves the straw in her mouth and inhales five shots of rum, vodka, and triple sec. She drinks it so fast her eyes burn.

"He didn't text you back?"

Jenny shakes her head and inhales more booze, her throat napalmed, her brain going thin from the fumes.

Her phone finally pings, and her eyes swan dive onto the screen.

`I thought you were more mature than this. Too bad,` Phil Fleischman's text says.

Jenny finishes the Hurricane in a numb fog. She wants to spear Rolando in the eye with her fruit toothpick. She wants to run away before Vanessa comes back. And she wishes like hell that Alex was here.

Rolando starts in. "Mercury is in retrograde, that's what it is. Don't say nothing important to nobody—" The fork next to Jenny flies across the table, puncturing the red leather near Rolando's head.

Rolando side-eyes the fork. "Maybe just don't drink no more."

But Jenny is not listening to him. She has even stopped drinking. Because she feels something behind her. An energy signature she knows. It's not Alex. And it's not Vanessa. Blue dust and the death card.

Phil Fleischman walks by her booth, wearing camel-colored slacks with a Gucci belt, his hair domed in a pompadour that almost hides his thinning front section. He is putting his phone back in his pocket. He does not notice Jenny.

"Sorry about that," he says. "A writer giving me trouble. You'd be surprised how unprofessional they can be."

"But not me, right?" The woman next to him laughs. She is petite, with soft auburn waves of hair, D-cup cleavage, smiling, well-adjusted. Rita Hayworth in a plum-blue silk dress. Her face is airy and guileless, like gravity has never given her reason to look down.

Jenny watches them sit at a table under the moose head. He pulls out her chair. She places a manuscript on the table. Phil Fleischman was planning dinner with Rita Hayworth at 7, and then drinks with Jenny at 11. She wonders if he is telling Rita the same thing he's been telling her.

Jenny scrambles to salvage any hope of being published.

`Sorry that was a joke meant for someone else,` she texts him.

She watches Phil glance at his phone, the lift of his eyebrows, the cold planes of his face. He taps at his screen. A moment later, her phone pings with his text.

`Ok.`

Is there ever any hope with an OK?

`I can't meet you this evening. But I could have coffee tomorrow,` she texts.

`Something has come up. Maybe next week.`

But the expression on his face tells her there will not be a next week.

Rejection 115 has an air of finality to it that breaks her in a way the other 114 before this have not. Jenny can't breathe. The floor is rotating. She grabs the edge of the table as the pictures begin to rattle against the wall.

"Jesus take the wheel." Rolando slides under the table.

Jenny cannot stop what happens. She tilts off balance, everything blurs, her future churning in lonely spirals that only run parallel to others, never crossing, never meeting. She will spend her life writing in her room, alone. The photos fly off the wall into a cyclone, diners drop their forks, their drinks, photos of priests and car salesmen hurtle around the room, bottles of liquor from the bar, Rolando's tarot cards, all converging above the table in the back.

There is an inch of air between Jenny's rear end and the seat now. Under the table, Rolando clamps onto her ankles, trying to stop her. Jenny shoves her messenger bag back on, thinking to weigh herself down. But she is unmoored, her lay lines tangled. She is cast into her own storm, her skirt billowing out, strands of black silk, her hair spreading out around her by centrifugal force, arms reaching for ballast and finding none.

Rita Hayworth screams, looking up as if Jenny is a winged monkey in the *Wizard of Oz*.

"Jenny Mandisi?" Phil Fleischman's voice slices through her delirium. "Is this some kind of stunt? Are you that desperate to be published?"

The drop is like the quiet of high altitude. Freefalling, ground reaching up to sock her in the jaw. The photos drop, the bottles too, exploding in a glitter of glass. Jenny lands a few tables away in a heap.

She forces herself up, aware she is bleeding where her legs hit the glass. People are running, limping, and using their walkers to get to the exit. She stumbles to the bathroom, into the stall, sliding to the floor. She stabs at her phone to text Alex.

`Please come get me. Bathroom. I'm in trouble.`

She searches her bag for the emergency pills. The ones that Dr. Lex prescribes. The ones Rolando calls horse sedatives and says she should slide up her rear end for faster effect. But she refuses to try that. Her hands shake as she twists the top, then grinds it the other way, unable to open it. With a pop it leaps off the px vial and a spray of blue pills arc up in the air, clatter off the rim of the toilet, plopping in the water. Her peace of mind sinks to the bottom of the bowl.

Jenny can't breathe, her lungs clamp, her stomach is being hit with a baseball bat. She knows this is a panic attack, but she can't stop it. Her phone beeps and she fumbles for it. She sees a text that doesn't make sense.

`We are done, freak.`

Alex wouldn't say that. Jenny peers at the screen. Of course she didn't send a text to Alex. Of course not. She sent it to the last person she'd been texting: Phil Fleischman. `Please come get me. Bathroom. I'm in trouble.` After she told him she wasn't a banjee ratchet ho and then floated to the ceiling and made his date piss her silk dress and then landed in the glass like Carrie at prom.

There is nothing Jenny can say to fix this. She forces herself to concentrate, to press the call button to Alex.

"Hey." Alex picks up right away. "Where are you?"

"Bathroom."

A minute later, black shoes appear on the tile floor, and the stall door swings open. He assesses her fleetly, his thoughts undistracted by emotion. "Scale of one to ten."

"Six," she says. As bad as this feels, she knows there is worse.

"Where's the diazepam?"

Jenny flaps her finger toward the toilet.

Alex bends down and picks up the empty bottle, reads the label carefully.

She is embarrassed to be seen like this. She tries to think of something to distract him. "Did you really rappel down a cliff today?"

"Yes." He doesn't look away from the bottle.

"Why didn't you say?"

"You have panic attacks." He checks something on his phone and then opens his EMT bag.

Jenny sees the silver watch on his wrist, hands unshaken. She can almost breathe.

"I'm not crazy," she says.

"That is correct." He swabs Jenny's inner arm. "You're psychokinetic, you can't handle alcohol…" He trails off for a moment as he draws clear liquid from a small vial into a syringe. "And you have the worst case of PTSD I've ever seen."

He slips the needle under her skin, finding a vein.

Jenny's teeth stop knocking together. Her chest unclenches. Her lungs sigh. She can breathe again. The baseball bat that has been bludgeoning her stomach stops. Her muscles go soft.

Jenny is like pudding now, unable to censor herself. The honey travels down her spine, filaments of light extend from her, wrapping around him, spinning a space where only they are. She knows that Alex cannot see it or feel it, that he is bound by inscrutable rules that govern him just as surely as Jenny's nightmares govern her. Perhaps this is as close as she comes to another. Maybe anything more is impossible. Still, for a moment she feels safe, feels the solitary core of iron that runs through him, something she can't pierce or understand. She only knows that she comes to ground when he is with her.

Her words leave her easily now. "Rolls took my phone and texted the book guy, the one I told you about. Total disaster. Must be Mercury in…something, I forget."

"Retrograde? Rolando is full of shit." Alex picks up Jenny's phone and scrolls through the screen. "You told this guy you were in trouble and needed help?" The tile under Alex's foot cracks with no warning.

"I thought I was texting you."

Alex scrolls further up the screen. "He wanted to meet you at King's Road. At eleven." The crack in the tile runs up the wall and hits the ceiling.

"I didn't say yes." Her blurred brain can't formulate why Alex is angry. Instead she says, "I'll never be published now. One hundred…fifteen rejections."

"Just keep writing," Alex says firmly, like he is done with the topic. He lifts Jenny up by the arm, and they move slowly out to the restaurant. She sees a swirl of red leather, broken glass. And Vanessa, blazing with fury.

"You pussy-mouthed mother-fucker!" Vanessa points a finger at Phil Fleischman.

He is still seated at the table. Rita Hayworth has disappeared.

Everyone else has run out. Jenny can't understand why he is still sitting there, except maybe Vanessa is blocking his way. Jenny wonders how her cousin noticed him at all, but then realizes her own thoughts made a map to him that Vanessa could not have missed.

"Have I done something to offend you, lady?" He smirks. And it is a really bad idea to smirk at Vanessa.

"How about not paying alimony? How about screwing my cousin over!"

"Your cousin? To whom do you refer?"

"That's it!"

The moose on the wall bursts into flames, its eyes melting, beloved moose smile ejecting sparks. Fur that is over fifty years old burns with an acrid, oily stink. Cocktail napkins erupt into fireworks, the remaining bottles of alcohol go Molotov. A few seconds later, the security cameras light up like Olympic torches.

Phil Fleischman shrieks as the chair behind him starts to burn, and his smirk vanishes.

Suspended above him in the air, slowly spinning, is one of Rolando's tarot cards. The death card. Phil Fleischman catches sight of Jenny, and his face mottles. "You! Fucking freak!"

Alex's foot comes down hard on the floor, and it fractures with a deep groan. A seismic shaking cleaves the carpet, the cement, the dirt and stone below. The fracture line shoots straight toward Phil Fleischman's table.

Alex loops his arm around Jenny's chest, like the safety bar on a roller coaster ride, pressing against the underside of her breasts, his palm and fingers under her arm, resting against her ribs. With no warning, Jenny is a million miles away from caring about her book or Phil Fleischman or the brimstone raining down on Cherry's Grill. Joy bubbles in her chest. A floaty feeling tingles in her toes, a sensation of lift.

"Nope," Alex says under his breath and squeezes her tightly, forcing her feet back on the ground. But the bubbles radiate through her, murmuring in a pleasant profusion of warmth. She looks at the scene from a distance. Her asshole cousin wielding fire in her corporate power-suit. Alex cracking the earth in two, pulling a hurricane of a Goth girl behind him. Rolando, the lousiest empath ever, leaking water under the table.

For just a sliver of a moment, Jenny smiles at Phil Fleischman, and she imagines that her black lipstick is smeared on her teeth, down her lips, that she must look like a specter of hell. Maybe she is. And she has friends you really shouldn't fuck with.

"Mandisi." Alex's voice clips the air. "Out. Now."

"Fine!" Vanessa throws her hands up like he's ruining her fun.

Alex pulls Jenny behind him, her legs languid. She watches as the table Phil Fleischman is sitting at slides into the fissure, the fire growing brighter. He claws at the air trying not to sink down with it. His hair-sprayed coxcomb bobs above the floor, and then she cannot see him at all.

The carpet recedes from Jenny's feet, then there's a bump, then she feels the smack of night air. The sky is dark now, inky black palm trees reaching for her. She hears Vanessa swearing and Rolando crying. There are police sirens approaching. Fire trucks too. Smoke the color of quicksilver snakes above Cherry's Grill.

Alex deposits Jenny in the ambulance passenger seat and walks around to the driver's side.

"I told you that guy is a wiener!" Vanessa yells, disappearing into her BMW.

"I told you Mercury is in retrograde!" Rolando cries, limping toward State Street.

Alex starts the engine and shakes his head, eyes crinkling at the corners.

"I told you to order milk."

"Glass" by Grace Rachow

A Turn with Worms

by Stephen T. Vessels

The coastline bristled with lights in the deepening dusk. Origin watched steel-sheened waters slide below as the pilot banked the shuttle toward the space port. The Channel Islands protruded from the Pacific like the knuckles of a drowned beast. Ten years since he'd been back. He didn't like the licensed sectors, Santa Barbara least of all. Origin didn't like any place where aliens had integrated with the human population. He liked still less the prospect of hunting here for a missing diplomat.

The pilot landed. Origin disembarked and headed for a waiting hover. The grey-blue sky was striated with pale bands of clouds. A cargo ship from Phisilon stood at the north end of the landing zone like a giant bronze dreidel balanced on its point.

The driver, a big fellow with square, expressionless features, held open the door.

"You know where I'm going?"

"I do, Detective."

Origin got in, tapped his wrist band and a holographic keypad appeared on his forearm. He typed in a number.

A voice from his ear bud responded, "Caldwell."

"Yeah, I'm here."

"Ian's waiting for you at . . . hang on." The line went silent. "Harry's Plaza Café."

Origin grimaced, watching shelf-like crystalline high-rises gleam by. "Why can't he meet me at the station?"

"I do not know."

"Ian Pine in a bar is not a good idea."

"It's his show, Nathan. Go see him."

"You're putting him in *charge?*"

The connection went dead. Origin sat back, groaning. He didn't mind the odd night out with his old partner, but he had no desire to run an investigation with him. The guy's entire life was a death-defying chemistry experiment.

Loretta Plaza sat like a wound amid the gleaming, pastel-hued high-rises. The antiquated strip mall had burned down in the early half of the twenty-first century, and been rebuilt by locals nostalgic for their beloved café. A hundred years later it was deemed a historical site, so the current denizens were stuck with it.

The driver pulled into the broad, uncovered lot where long rows of hovers were parked. A few locals in swank attire strolled along the L-shaped row of shops, looking in windows. A more pedestrian example of pre-interstellar architecture could not have been singled out for preservation.

Harry's Plaza Café hunkered at the elbow of the strip. The driver let Origin out by the entrance. Origin followed a couple of high hats through the glass door. The interior was dimly lit, red leather booths and wood tables extending ahead, paralleled on the left by a long wood bar lined with round-topped stools. Just inside the door, to the left, the old open-faced kitchen was preserved as a curiosity but no longer in use. Everything faithful, supposedly, to the bar's original layout. The walls were bedecked with photos of famous patrons of times past, their identities long forgotten.

The place was crowded, all tables occupied. Origin didn't see any skitters or worms, which was a relief, but he didn't see Ian either. He went through the entryway between the bar and the defunct kitchen into the vast back room, where the lighting was brighter. Half-circle booths lined the left wall, round-topped tables filling the floor area. Across the room to the right was the famous hyper-field wall, which supposedly afforded a muddy view of a sister establishment on the planet humans called Wax, home world of the worms. Origin made out vague lumpy figures amid smeary zones of illumination.

On this side of the wall the tiny hat brigade was out in force. A dozen or more men wore minuscule fedoras, bowlers, and top hats affixed to their heads at diverse angles. Pin-striped suits were back in style, pants cut short at the knees. The fashion choices of the wealthy had long since ceased to fascinate Origin. Some of the women who knew how to dress with style were interesting to look at.

With displeasure he noted the presence of aliens.

The bar wrapped around from the front room in a U. A few people in Old West attire stood there. Origin contemplated the figure of a slim cowgirl in a snug, sequined outfit until he noticed she'd had leg augmentations. Her feet had been replaced with hooves. Her companions had undergone similar alterations. A couple had tails sticking out of their pants. One woman's swished as she laughed. Origin had heard about centaurs but hadn't seen any before.

He spotted Ian at a half-circle booth. Age had beaten him up some. The lines in his round, jovial face had deepened, and he'd put on weight since Origin had last seen him, but he was still a fashion hound. He had on a shimmering black silk jacket and a red shirt embroidered with peacocks. On the table in front of him was a steel decanter and a half-full martini glass. Also a neat line of pills: two yellow, three red, one white. He popped a red one as Origin sat down.

"Caldwell says you're lead."

Pine issued a wheezy, reticent laugh. "How are you, Nate? Good to see you."

Origin resigned himself to the situation. His old partner was well in his cups. "Nothing ever happens simply with you, does it." Or sanely.

Pine rocked, resettling himself, a barbed grin fixed and inscrutable.

A waitress lean as a coat hanger came over. "Need a menu?" she asked Origin.

He shook his head. He recognized her. She was famous for having worked at Harry's for something like seventy years. She'd had another body rebuild.

"He drinks Scotch," Ian said before she got away. "Neat and unpeated. And I'll take another couple of these." He shook the decanter at her.

The waitress cast a glance ceilingward and left.

Origin stared placidly at Pine. "Am I just going to sit here while you render yourself unconscious?"

Ian popped a yellow pill and winked at him. "Have to be in top form tonight. I'm not the one you need to talk to." He signaled someone. A grey-haired person chatting with the centaurs waved back. He traded a parting joke with the behoofed woman Origin had eyed and wound his way toward them through the tables.

Ian stood up to let the man slide in.

"Interesting group," the newcomer said. "Rodeo performers. About to head off-world on tour."

Origin glanced back. "Why did they do that to themselves?"

"I guess they like it," the newcomer said.

"Captain Hieronymus Reed," Ian said, before the silence stretched awkwardly, "meet Senior Detective Nathan Origin. Hieron is captain of the *Lamplighter*, Nate."

"I know who you are," Origin said. "You're a privateer, Captain, a pirate in a bigger sea."

Reed met Origin's critical gaze placidly. "A rose by any other name."

"Why am I talking to this guy?" Origin asked Ian.

"Because you don't know what you're doing," the captain said.

"What's that supposed to mean?"

Reed leaned close. "You might want to keep your voice down."

Origin sniffed. "You might want to answer me."

"You think you're looking for one missing diplomat of the Interplanetary Foreign Services."

Origin stared at Ian. "You *told* him?"

"He knew. That's why I called you."

Origin scrutinized Reed. A worm wriggled up the aisle close by. Origin caught the cautionary look in Reed's eyes. The worm flopped its fore-end against their table. It had a miniature top hat affixed at a tilt above its watery eye clusters. It's grey, wrinkled skin glistened atypically with perspiration. Wet, gargly noises issued from its mouth hole.

In his ear bud Origin heard, "Knowing of waste depository place, obsequious?" The worm extended an inquiring pseudopod toward Ian's gimlet.

Ian slid the martini glass out of reach and pointed toward the double doors at the inner end of the room. "The one you're looking for is through there, at the back of the banquet room."

The worm looked where Ian pointed. "Of thanking, obsequious," it said, and flopped away. Its movements were irregular and sluggish. The thing was smashed out of its alien gourd.

Reed leaned close to Origin. "Imagine how much better it would be," he said quietly, "if you knew what you were really doing."

Origin scanned the room more attentively, affecting a casual attitude. He counted nine aliens—seven worms and two skitters. "I'm listening."

"You think you're looking for one person."

"I'm not?"

Ian leaned forward. "In the past twelve weeks, seventeen people have been reported missing, last seen in this bar. No one can conduct an official investigation here because technically it's no-man's land, neither Wax nor Earth."

"The hyper-field wall," Origin said.

Ian nodded. "An official investigation would involve the ambassadorial services, and they are pointedly keeping their distance."

Reed lifted his chin at the hyper-field wall. "What do you know about that?"

The view clarified briefly, and Origin had a fleeting impression of worms lounging on mushy sofas. "Well, I know you could power about twelve cities on what it takes to maintain it. Theoretically I could walk through it and step out on Ishfa-C—on Wax . . ." Origin frowned. He thought he saw humans, too. "Setting aside that I'd need an interplanetary passport to do that, the thing is unstable, so I'd probably come out with my liver where my brain's supposed to be, looking like a wad of offal." He turned back to the captain. "It's an expensive oddity, an art installation, diplomatic gift of the worms."

"That's a socially inappropriate way to refer to them."

"I'm sorry, Visiting Invertebrate Persons, that better?"

"VIPs is acceptable now, I'm told."

"That what you call them?"

The captain's eyes acquired a transient gleam. "No, I call them worms." He sat back and watched Origin.

"What's the most important thing we get from trade with the worms?" Ian asked.

Origin considered the question. He had a sneaking apprehension that he was about to get into something over his head. "Regestive conditioning."

"Look around," the captain said.

Origin held the captain's gaze a couple of beats before doing as he directed. He saw people sitting at tables, having dinner, and drinking. The worms were all gathered in the far left corner, near the hyper-field, sprawled on divans around a low, oblong table. The skitters were suspended from self-spun hammocks at the bar.

Origin glanced back at the captain.

"Keep looking."

Origin honed his attention, table to table. He stopped on a foursome, two men and two women, peered at their food. "What are they eating?"

"Looks like desiccated snail carcasses from Batrique," Ian said.

"Those are snails?"

"They kind of look like snails when they're alive," the captain said, "if snails had wings and teeth."

"They're a delicacy on Batrique," Ian said.

Origin stared at his tablemates. "The operative phrase there is 'on Batrique.' For Enchimites."

"Or humans," Ian said, "who work for the Department of Interplanetary Affairs and have undergone regestive conditioning."

"Those people are diplomats?" Origin watched Ian and the captain shake their heads.

"See that little vial of white stuff on their table?" Ian asked.

Origin spotted a slender, urn-shaped vial full of a substance that had a faintly opalescent glow.

Ian signaled the waitress. "We'd like the alternate menu."

A faint distaste crossed her features. She brought a leather-bound menu that she slapped in front of Ian and strode away. He tossed it to Origin.

Unpronounceable words accompanied a visual gallery of

dishes. Nothing in the menu looked remotely edible. It was hard to distinguish animal from vegetable, and pretty much everything was the wrong color.

"I don't get it."

"Regestive conditioning is based on worm biology," Ian said. "They're born space farers. Their digestive system is naturally regestive; it accommodates almost anything. For us to acquire that ability, we have to rewire our DNA, with viral cultures spliced with the worm equivalent of DNA. Only the worms have the technology to make those cultures, which they ain't sharing. So unless you qualify for an interplanetary passport or work for the government or have a wealthy sponsor, forget it. And if you're not traveling off-world, you don't need it.

"However, the worms have a non-viral concoction that, if you drink it, mimics regestive conditioning for about six hours."

Origin studied the menu. Between pictures of dubious comestibles was one of a vial, like the one at the far table, filled with white fluid.

"You're telling me that rich idiots," he read the price of the white stuff, "*very* rich idiots, come here to eat things that should never go anywhere near a human mouth."

"Thrill-seekers," the captain said. "But that's the wrong question."

"I'm not sure I want to know the right one."

"It isn't what the stuff is to us, it's what it is to them."

Another presence arrived at the table. Origin found himself confronted by a formidable woman with turbulent black hair and sharp, intelligent eyes. She wore a form-fitting black gown that cascaded irregularly with multi-hued shimmers, and had a very large python draped around her neck.

She made to sit down next to Origin, and he scooted aside. The woman winked at him. He could have sworn the snake did too, and scooted yet farther, making the captain move.

"Does my little friend frighten you, Detective?"

"Little? That thing could swallow a cat."

"Oh, it can swallow things much larger than cats."

The python swung its head toward Origin and flicked its tongue. Origin shrank away.

"Did you get it, Silver?" Ian asked.

"Mm-hmm." She passed a folded piece of paper across the table, gave Origin a mischievous look, and departed.

Origin scooted away from the captain and resettled himself. "Does everyone in this place know who I am?"

"Only the ones who need to," Ian said.

"What's that?" Origin extended a finger at the scrap of paper.

"The exact time that the hyper-field will stabilize."

"What's it give us?" the captain asked.

Ian unfolded the note. He popped another yellow pill and washed it down with the remains of his Gimlet before answering.

"Seven seconds, in about twenty minutes."

The captain made a grim, grumbling noise in his throat.

What they had in mind began to assemble itself in Origin's understanding. "Hey, if you two think I'm going over there— seven *seconds?*"

"We'll have to be quick," the captain allowed.

"Let me get this straight. You think I'm going to hop halfway across the galaxy with you, rescue seventeen people, and hop back, all in seven seconds."

"Not exactly," Ian said.

"I imagine not."

"Some things have to be done off the books, Nate, or they never get done. You know that."

Ian's eyes, apart from being glazed, seemed to be operating independently of each other. Origin didn't know how he was managing to sit upright, let alone carry on a conversation. "Here's what I know: If what you two think is true, it's time to get Interplanetary Affairs involved." He tapped his wrist band.

The captain covered it with his hand. "Wouldn't it be great if someone had a plan." He fixed Origin with a hard gaze.

Origin pulled his arm away. Ian's seat was empty. Origin spotted him teetering toward the bar. He had to be the least sober person in the room, and he was running this operation. Whatever the hell it was.

Ian started chatting up the curvaceous centaur who had attracted Origin's attention earlier. Whatever he was saying drew growing disapproval from the males in the party. One in particular—a tall, brutish type with abundant muscles and little in the way of a forehead. If anyone was going to keep this farce from descending into chaos, Origin saw it would likely have to be him.

He headed to the bar. The curvaceous centaur seemed amused by Ian. Origin suspected she might be equally amused to see him stomped into a carpet stain.

"I bet those hooves give you great purchase when you're riding one of these broncos," Origin heard him say.

The beefy centaur reached for Ian. Origin stepped between them, banged his whiskey glass on the bar top and called to the bartender. "Hey, I've got a problem."

The bartender gave him a weary look. "Yeah, what's that?"

"My glass is empty. There's supposed to be Scotch in it, old and unpeated."

"That's the spirit, Nate." Ian slapped him on the shoulder.

Origin leaned close and said quietly in Ian's ear, "What the hell are you doing?"

His old partner's response could not have been more unexpected. Ian seized Origin in a firm embrace and kissed him, full-mouthed, tongue included.

Origin hadn't been kissed by anyone since his wife dumped him. In the behemoth tangle of signals and reactions blundering through his psyche, the only response he could muster was to ease free of Ian's embrace and regard the wonder of him in comprehensive bewilderment.

Ian winked at him. "Roll with it." For no discernible reason, he ducked.

Origin caught the slap intended for Ian. The sexy centaur had a mean right cross. "Fuck *you!*" she shouted, and spun about to kick Ian. He slipped aside and her hoof caught Origin in the gut, flinging him backward into Beefy, who shoved him aside with an incoherent roar, and reached for Ian.

"*Bitch!*" Ian shouted at Sexy. "You leave my boyfriend alone!"

Origin grabbed Ian by the collar and pulled him beyond Beefy's reach. Fists started flying in *absurdium delicto*. The brawl communicated outward from its senseless hub like a dividing cell. One of the centaurs clocked a bouncer, who sprawled backward onto a dining table, sending an "alternate" dish of something like writhing cilia spraying outward across other diners.

"You're fucking paying for that!" one of the sybaritic diners yelled at the bouncer.

The skitters climbed their hammocks to get clear of the violence. Some patrons scrambled for the exit or any oasis of safety, others joined in the fracas with gusto. Origin propelled Ian the length of the bar to the hallway adjacent the hyper-field wall that led to the men's room.

Ian stumbled away from him, reeling to face a full-length, gilt-framed mirror. Confronted with his own reflection, his eyes went wide.

"You again!" he screamed. He grabbed the mirror by its frame. "You're not getting away this time!"

"Ian!" Origin shouted.

Ian wrenched the mirror free of the wall. "Got you now, you fuck!" He turned and toppled face forward onto the mirror, which shattered. "Take that, you fucking shit bastard fuck!"

Origin yanked him to his feet. Someone grabbed Origin's shoulder, and he swung around in a crouch. It was the captain. He took hold of Origin's chin and turned his attention down the length of the hyper-field wall. Origin saw three worms flit through the wall, quick as lightning.

"Time to go," Reed said. He plunged through the hyper-field, dragging Origin with him.

Reality disintegrated, turned inside out, and stretched like taffy. When it stabilized again, Origin promptly vomited and pissed himself. He barely managed to keep his sphincter closed.

"Fuck me sideways," the captain wheezed. Reed was leaning against a wall, gathering himself. They were in a dimly lit oval corridor. The way behind them was sealed by a flat, grey barrier.

Origin climbed to his feet. The curve of the floor challenged his balance. He felt heavier than he had in the bar. "Where—" Origin retched again, unproductively. "What the earthly fuck?"

"We went through the hyper-field," the captain managed.

"We're on Wax?"

Before Reed could answer, Ian stumbled through the wall and fell in a heap. Origin tried to help him up, but Ian slipped from his grasp and fell back down.

"Fuck, fuck, fuck, fuckity fucking fuck," Ian said. He had not made it through the hyper-field intact. He was missing his left foot. Blood spewed from the stump in pulsating streams.

Origin shed his jacket, took off his shirt, tore off a sleeve, and tied it around Ian's calf. "Find me something to tighten this with," he told the captain.

Reed took a collapsible combat baton from his back pocket and gave it to Origin.

Nathan slid it under the knot in the shirt sleeve and twisted it until the bleeding stopped. "Hold this."

Reed knelt and held the baton while Origin tore the other sleeve off of his shirt and tied it around the makeshift tourniquet to hold it in place.

"Goddamit." Ian looked at his stump. "That was a brand new foot."

No hyper-field was apparent the way they'd come, just the slate-grey barrier, a little below eye level on which a glowing rectangle shown, complex in its composition. Origin stepped close. It was a miniature hologram of the tableau he'd seen through the hyper-field, worms lounging on sofas, humans in chairs. The hologram was static.

"What is this?"

"What?" Ian pushed himself up.

"Some kind of projection. It's like what we saw on the other side."

Origin pulled his jacket back on, helped Ian stand on his remaining foot, and they followed the captain up the corridor. Some distance along it curved left and opened onto a broad, oval room similar to the one depicted in the hologram but more elaborate. The smell was a disgusting mix of excrement and something like marzipan. Worms were in fact lounging there, not on sofas but in cushioned depressions in the floor, which itself was slightly concave.

Amid the worms a number of humans sat at tables, here and there sipping from tall, slender containers like metal champagne flutes. It was difficult for Origin to process.

The humans seemed stoned or somehow subdued. Origin registered that they were all naked from the waist down, and had long, flexible tubes descending from between their buttocks. The worms held the other ends of the tubes in their pseudopods and appeared to be sucking from them. They seemed oblivious to the presence of Origin and his companions.

Ian grabbed the back of an empty chair and shooed Origin away. "Help Hieron."

The captain pulled the tubes out of two humans seated near each other.

Origin went to him, at a loss. "You said something about a plan." He resisted the urge to retch again.

"We can't save all of them," the captain said. "I'm getting my crewmates out of here. Find your diplomat. We get him out, I.F.S. will be forced to act. Here." He gave Origin a glass ampule. "This will help bring him 'round."

Origin called up Simon Thornhill's image on his wrist monitor, went table to table, scrutinizing faces. The humans were in such reduced states that their faces had become waxen and generic. He almost passed beyond the diplomat before realizing he'd found him. He pulled the tube from the man's rectum, looking away as he did so, then broke the ampule the captain had given him under the man's nose. Thornhill blinked and began to rouse from his stupor.

"Nate, give me a hand," Ian called. Origin watched him dump the viscous contents of a champagne flute and clip off the foot of the flute with a pocket snip. Then he placed the flute, mouth down, on the floor.

Origin helped him up. "What are you doing?"

"Hold me steady." Ian positioned the stump of his left foreleg over the stem of the flute and put his weight on it, forcing the stem up into his leg.

Origin winced. "How can you fucking do that?"

"Yeah, it'd probably hurt if I could feel anything. I need to be able to stand." He pushed away from Origin and stood on his own. "That'll work. Let's move."

Ian hobbled over to Thornhill and went through the diplomat's jacket. He found the passport and pocketed it, muttered, "Arrogant bastards."

The disconnected worms began to rouse. One of them burbled something Origin's translator couldn't make sense of.

Origin and Ian, Thornhill between them, made their way up another oval corridor at the end of the room opposite where they'd entered, arriving at length in a vast enclosure that Origin recognized to be the hangar deck of an interstellar vessel. Ranks of docked passenger and cargo transports stretched into far, beshadowed distances.

Origin looked up and stopped in his tracks, awestruck.

"What?" Ian asked.

A silvery, gleaming array of winding slides and tube-ways spanned the reaches above, like the lacework of a giant weaver. The complexity of the structure was breathtaking. "My God. It's so—"

"Beautiful?" the captain said. "Yeah, I know. Get your passports ready."

"I don't have a passport," Origin said.

"I slipped it in your inner jacket pocket," Ian told him.

Origin felt around, pulled out a gleaming, freshly minted interplanetary passport. He opened it. A holographic photo of the beefy centaur beamed back at him. "I do not remotely look like this guy."

"We all look alike to the worms," Ian said.

Origin was still dumbfounded by their surroundings. "This is a ship. We're inside a ship. Where the hell are we? I thought we were supposed to come out on Wax."

"It's a worm ship orbiting Earth," the captain said.

"But the hyper-field—"

"Is bullshit," Reed said. "Nobody has the tech to stabilize a dimensional rift between a bar on Earth and someplace halfway across the fucking galaxy. No one we've run into yet, anyway. Reason it out. If the worms could do that, what use would they have for the largest interstellar fleet of any space-faring species? It's just some little phase link they set up between the bar and their ship."

Origin stared around at the hangar. "It's bullshit?"

"Yep."

"And this whole thing is just so they can, what, suck the— you've got to be kidding me."

"Two things you want to know about worms. One is they can move a lot faster than they let on. The other is they have no fucking concept of restraint when it comes to satisfying their appetites." The captain pointed up. "Here we go."

Worms slid onto the hangar deck from several of the looping slides. The captain was right, they moved faster than Origin had supposed they could. Their undulations were much more economical and adroit than he had previously witnessed.

The captain tapped his wrist com. "Hieron, here," he said quietly. "Come in, *Lamplighter*."

Origin couldn't hear the other end of the exchange.

"Got a fix on me?"

One of the worms slid toward the group ahead of the others. It had red and green marks on its flanks, like paint strokes slashed with a fat brush, distinguishing it as the superior of a worm constabulary force.

"Breach A.S.A.P.," the captain said.

Several of the worms following the leader bore in their pseudopodia the plasma-burst weapons humans called squash blossoms.

Ian left Thornhill with Origin and hobbled forward to confront the lead worm. Origin recognized his partner at work, the man who would never fail you in a foxhole. He could be in the most consuming state of chemically distorted consciousness imaginable, and when urgency required it, manifest composure and competence. Ian held open a diplomatic passport for the worm to see, signaling Origin and Reed, with an upward gesture of his free hand, to display theirs as well. Origin held up his stolen passport.

"This is Ambassadorial Liaison Simon Thornhill," Ian said, waving back at Thornhill. "We are his aides. Occupants of this ship have committed high crimes and violated the Interplanetary Treaty of Phisolon cum Alpha. Stand down your agents. This ship and its contents are hereby seized for examination and all occupants will submit to questioning."

The lead worm's sloshy vocalizations translated in Origin's ear as, "Your authority is void making. You board this vessel illegal. Warrant of Ishfa-C require."

"We can board any vessel in Earth space to intervene in crimes committed against humans. And we didn't board this vessel, we tripped through your phony fucking hyper-shield wall in Harry's Café."

The worm said something that translated as, "Make lip music to my bulbosity."

An explosion thundered through the vault of the hull. A hole appeared in the hull when a large, ragged disc collapsed onto the flight deck. Crew members of the *Lamplighter* poured through the breach, heavily armed.

"Now," Reed said.

One of the worm guard aimed its squash blossom at Thornhill. Ian leapt forward, performed a kind of pirouette on his makeshift peg foot, and kicked the weapon. The plasma bead went wide and burst against the hull of a freighter, leaving a radial, smoldering black scar.

The situation swiftly deteriorated into chaos. Plasma beads and blaster bursts sliced back and forth through the hangar bay. Origin aimed to wound and not kill as he ducked and dodged across the flight deck. The captain was less restrained.

He seared a worm straight in its face. The worm vomited out its guts across the floor. Origin nearly fell, slipping through the glop.

They made it to the breach. Two of the captain's crew took hits, helping their impaired crewmates. As soon as they were all through the breach, the umbilicus sealed and retracted toward the *Lamplighter*. Through the transparent wall of the umbilicus, Origin saw the sleek, horizontally ribbed lance of the *Lamplighter*, its flanks emblazoned with fire-breathing dragon skulls.

Several worms were sucked into space before they got a containment field activated. Origin looked on grimly as the spaced worms writhed spasmodically and went still.

Medical teams awaited them inside the *Lamplighter*.

"Get that bleeding stopped!" the captain shouted.

"I'm trying!" a med tech working on one of the wounded crewmen shouted back.

Other medical personnel led off Thornhill and the *Lamplighter* crew members they'd freed from the worms' perverse feeding lair.

"I hope we haven't started a war," Origin said.

"You'd rather we'd left them there to be sucked on like milkshakes?" Reed said.

Origin didn't answer. "Back in the bar, you said I asked the wrong question."

"What?"

"That white stuff—you said it isn't what it is to us, it's what it is to them."

"So?"

"What is it? To them?"

The captain gave Origin an angry scowl. "Seasoning."

Origin went with Ian to a medical bay.

"We can rebuild the foot," a doctor told Ian. "There's so much tissue damage, though, I'd rather amputate above the knee and rebuild the entire lower leg."

"I leave it to you, Doctor," Ian said.

"And then I think we might have a talk about your drug and alcohol intake."

"Sure, we can talk all you want."

When they were alone, Ian asked Origin, "Did I kiss you back there?"

"Yes."

"Oh. Sorry."

"It's okay."

"I do love you, you know."

"I love you too. But I like women."

"They have drugs for that. Or I could undergo augmentations."

"Ian, if we got involved, I'd have to kill you."

Ian's mouth twisted in resignation. "I miss being your partner."

"I do not miss being yours."

The two friends fell silent, looking out the view port together, watching the inscrutable heavens drift by through an incomprehensible universe.

Ted Chiles

Ted came to creative writing after moving to California in 2003. With a Ph.D. in Economics, he taught economics at the undergraduate and graduate levels. In 2013, he completed an MFA in fiction from Spalding University. Chiles' fiction has been published in print and online and consists of short stories and flash fiction. His style varies from realism to magical realism to speculative fiction. He also has published creative nonfiction, adapted a novella for the stage, and written two ten-minute plays, one of which was produced in Santa Barbara. Originally from the Rust Belt, Chiles lives in Santa Barbara with a writer and two cats.

Chella Courington

Chella is a writer and teacher. With a Ph.D. in American and British Literature and an MFA in Poetry, she is the author of five poetry and four flash fiction chapbooks. Her poetry and flash fiction appear in numerous anthologies and journals, including *The Los Angeles Review, Spillway, SmokeLong Quarterly,* and *The Collagist*. Originally from the Appalachian South, Courington lives in California with another writer and two cats. For more information, visit chellacourington.net.

Nicholas Deitch

Nick is a writer, teacher, architect, and activist. Originally from Los Angeles, California, he now lives in Ventura, with his wife, Diana. He is an annual participant at the Santa Barbara Writer's Conference. He has been published in the London literary journal, *Litro,* and is currently writing his first novel, *Death and Life in the City of Dreams*, a story about a dying city and those who struggle to save it.

Lisa Lamb

Lisa was born and raised in the UK, where she had her first career as a pop star. She has written multiple global hit songs (published by Warner Chappell) and worked as a copywriter for a big branding agency. She has also owned her own audio branding business, published a nonfiction book on stellar nucleosynthesis, and is currently teaching K-6 music in a Santa Barbara public elementary school.

Tom Layou

Tom lives in Alaska and has had journalistic work published in the *Anchorage Daily News*. Tom is a regular attendee of the Santa Barbara Writers Conference, where he won an award for best nonfiction at the age of eighteen. More recently he has been published in *Luna Review* and the *Santa Barbara Literary Journal*. He pays his rent selling legal cannabis. Twitter: @tomlayou_writer, Instagram: tomlayou, Facebook: Tom Layou.

Christine Casey Logsdon

Christine earned her degree in English Literature from UCSB in 1991, and owns and manages a technical consulting company. She has lived in Santa Barbara with her husband and extended family for decades, and edits both fiction and nonfiction. Christine writes fiction of all lengths, and is currently editing her contemporary Southern novel and a dramatic suspense novel.

Shelly Lowenkopf

Shelly lives, writes, and teaches in Santa Barbara. Former editor-in-chief of four book publishers; ran the LA office for what was then Dial, Dell, Delacorte Press. Had an editorial hand in three genre magazines and one literary journal. Reviewed fiction for major metropolitan dailies, taught at graduate, undergraduate levels for thirty-five years. Did all this with a BA and abundant chutzpah.

Matthew J. Pallamary

Matt is an award-winning author, editor, and shamanic explorer who has authored fourteen books. His most recent novel, *AfterLife: The Adventures of a Lost Soul,* is an occult thriller that explores what happens when someone drinks alcohol to the point of blacking out and is inspired by real life events, William Peter Blatty's *The Exorcist,* and the dynamics of demonic possession. Matt has taught a Phantastic Fiction workshop at the Southern California Writers' Conference in San Diego and Los Angeles, and at the Santa Barbara Writers Conference for close to thirty years.
www.mattpallamary.com

Max Talley

Max is a writer and artist who was born in New York City and now resides in Southern California. Talley's fiction and essays have appeared in *Del Sol Review, Fiction Southeast, Gravel, Hofstra University – Windmill, Bridge Eight, Litro Magazine,* and *The Opiate,* among others. His near future novel, *Yesterday We Forget Tomorrow,* was published in 2014, and he teaches a writing workshop at the Santa Barbara Writers Conference. More art and writings at www.maxdevoetalley.com.

Grace Rachow

Grace Rachow is an artist, a dog lover, and the director of the Santa Barbara Writers Conference. She has worked as an editor, writer, and freight handler.

John Reed

John's years as an Army Intelligence officer have given him more than enough background for his four espionage novels: *Thirteen Mountain, Dark Forest, Shadow White as Stone,* and *The Kingfisher's Call.* John is famous for conducting the Pirate Workshop at the Santa Barbara Writers Conference, and his poetry has appeared in more than 50 literary magazines and journals. Follow him online at www.johnreedbooks.com.

Dennis Russell

Santa Barbara-based singer-songwriter Dennis Russell has released 5 albums: *My Little World, Primitive-Acoustic-Sensitive-Singer-Songwriter-Type-Guy, Golden, 7 of Townes,* and *Plain: Primitive-Acoustic-Sensitive-Singer-Songwriter-Type-Guy, Too.* He has also self-published a book of short stories, *That Fourth of July,* and a book of poetry, *Surfer Songs.*

For concert dates and recordings, visit dennisrussellroad.com

Stephen T. Vessels

Stephen is a Thriller Award nominated author of science fiction, dark fantasy, and cross-genre ficiton. His stories have appeared in *Ellery Queen Mystery Magazine*, and collections from Grey Matter Press and ShadowSpinners Press. His story collection, *The Mountain & The Vortex and Other Tales* was released by Muse Harbor Publishing. He has written art and music reviews for the *Santa Barbara Independent* and is a published poet and visual artist. You can visit him at www.stephentvessels.com.

Silver Webb

Silver is the Editrix of the *Santa Barbara Literary Journal* as well as a food writer for *Food & Home*. Silver is a freelance editor and designer with a habit of writing novels. You can see more about Silver's writing and adventures at silverwebb.com or @bakery_babe.

Borda Books

www.sblitjo.com
www.bordabooks.com
All titles available on amazon.com

Santa Barbara Literary Journal,
Volume 1: Andromeda, June 2018

Santa Barbara Literary Journal,
Volume 2: Cor Serpentis, December 2018

Hurricanes & Swan Songs, April 2019

Made in the USA
Columbia, SC
05 April 2019